THE
MARQUEE MURDERS

A JONAS KIRK MYSTERY

DICK SNYDER

authorHOUSE®

AuthorHouse™
1663 Liberty Drive
Bloomington, IN 47403
www.authorhouse.com
Phone: 1 (800) 839-8640

Published by AuthorHouse 10/23/2019

ISBN: 978-1-7283-3238-3 (sc)
ISBN: 978-1-7283-3236-9 (hc)
ISBN: 978-1-7283-3237-6 (e)

Library of Congress Control Number: 2019916749

ACKNOWLEDGEMENTS

As always, fiction emerges from minds well apart from that of the author. I've been especially supported in creating this manuscript by the following, and I deeply appreciate their efforts.

Jym Thrailkill read the manuscript several times, making key, helpful suggestions about plot, dialogue and narrative. His was a remarkable and highly beneficial effort which affected content, tone and tempo.

Ken Sorenson brought an energy which bolstered mine, thoughtfully offering some plot lines and lending his musical expertise to some of the narrative. His enthusiasm is infectious.

Linda Snyder somehow found time to read and re-read copy as it emerged and as it was edited. Her efforts always make the storyline more coherent. She also keeps me calm and thoughtful, not an inconsiderable task.

As always, I am fully and solely responsible for the fiction you are about to read. Enjoy. Dick

CONTENTS

INTRODUCTION

In Woodland Park, movies are a big thing. Lazy nights and weekly features on murder mysteries intrigue locals. But when film plots begin to connect to real life death in the parking lot, Lt. Chester Devlin is perplexed. Jonas Kirk is curious. They, local attorney, Roger Blaisdell and newbie cop, Oliver Grant, search for connections.

An athletic couple, the Gordons, continue to grapple with their crumbling marriage while Kirk and his romantic partner, Sharon Cunningham, speculate on likely motives for a serial killer.

Geraldine Wright's gym workouts produce tips that lead to insurance salesmen, drug peddlers and a weaponry expert. Devlin's observations produce a muddle of evidence that seems compelling. Kirk proposes solutions that identify a killer. But is it the right script?

RIVOLI
1
THE WORRY

Kirk drifted slowly in the balloon, felt it rise as the burner sent hot air into the canopy, shifting his horizon, floating higher into the haze. Securely settled in the basket, he took occasional looks at the earth below, changed the view with a mere thought, recalled satisfying memories of his risky life choices...a young man's privilege. The images...fulfilling. The risks...acceptable.

Winding now through wispy strands of cloudy puffery, his thoughts touched on faces as subtly diverse as swirling fall leaves. There...a rough talking drunk in a train; a bulky blonde wandering away from his twin; a tortured face topped with a circle of holiness; a baker with a mouth full of peanut butter icing. They were his responsibility, the product of his calculated justice, set into reality by his action, justified by his perception of the world about him and his belief that at least one human settlement deserved his attention: Woodland Park.

Birds flew by towing banners, some large, some too small to read. The years presented themselves, each filling a part of a decade...and he found himself changing perspectives. At first, he became youthfully estranged in a community which he had treated as an accomplice in his parent's tragic loss. An image of drugs at Emily Horner's party flashed into view, then disappeared. His chance encounter with Sergeant Chester Devlin blared in his mind like sounds from a carnival. The balloon rose a bit more, allowed him to create a bond with Devlin, revealed a new focus in life. Personal loss, once so efficient in wiping clean his empathy, now scrubbed him into an intimate remake. Homicide became his focus. Sorting it out one way or another formed a fixation. Sometimes, he worked in tandem with Devlin. Sometimes he worked between the policeman's lines, focusing on the need for justice and just how he might execute it. Execution indeed. One way or the other, he thought, he had a responsibility.

He floated, passed over his little town whose faces popped up about him from moment to moment and there in the cloud forming just above, and a little beyond, she appeared. Classic face, glittering eyes that narrowed from moment to moment, a body that flowed indistinctly into the folds of her wispy gown: Sharon Cunningham. As could only happen in dreams, he became flooded with her scent, however distant it might have been, remembered her touch from a time he could not place, knew that even without recognition by others, theirs was a bond that time strengthened. In his dreaming, a voice told him she was dangerous, but then her imagery overwhelmed his caution once again. Whatever size the brain, the heart was always larger. Sharon Cunningham, his lover now formed as Lady Justice. He, Mr. Scales, besotted, an instrument of action. As in a movie, slides flashed through the lighted screen, introducing faces, characters and teaser scenes, finding the two of them entwined in cinematic imagery.

The credits rolled and the film ended. Director: Orson Welles.

Confusion now as clouds darkened. A face appeared, then another. Memory tags grew larger, sadder in their facial expression, some overwhelmed by fright. He glanced at each and mentally popped the image into the benign peace of a corpse in a coffin. Right where they belonged...he reassured himself. Mr. Scales was doing it right. He protected Woodland Park. He remained justified. He remained Jonas Kirk.

And now, the balloon settled. Earth recaptured his sense of proportion. He stirred, awakened, still savoring his dream, wanting the movie to play on. Circling into reality. Where was he landing?

RIVOLI
2
SCREENING ROOM

(Late February)

Steve Gordon sat quietly in the dark, slowly dropping the derringer from palm to palm, the rhythm soothing his restlessness, his mind reflecting on the film, it's purpose, it's victims.

ZODIAC. It stirred him, touched his gut. Smart people helpless. Cops befuddled. A serial killer without a pattern. Murder free of charge. Unpredictable. Unidentifiable. Hmmmpphh.

He reached out, touched the "lights up" button on his console, sighed as the screen receded, the reality of life slowly eclipsing his film imaginings. He felt the weight of the derringer, now in his left hand, its twin still in the locked box. Looked at it. So tidy. Two barrels fitted for 22L bullets, precisely loaded, so easily fired. He renewed the rhythm amid reflection, the weight slapping itself into his hands, each palm cradling, nestling, restlessly caressing its lethal mass. Boredom controlled his life... highs gone, lows pervasive. Needed something new, a challenge, a life reset that would test his skills, use his knowledge. He let the warm weight float back and forth... back and forth.

Those bullets in the two chambers taunted him. What were they? Scrap metal taking up space or messages waiting to be delivered...and then what? Could they bring excitement to his daily workouts, curtail his wife Eleanor's distancing...her hostility? Just how might that happen? He continued to consider. Maybe the two of them were just another version of a sad romantic couples drama, each act sharpening their disjointed lives, sparse dialogue flowing past one another, isolated wanderings that carefully avoided crossing paths. Eh? Was she a promise for the future or a dead weight dragging him into a mud pit? Dead weight? Interesting thought.

He let his mind wander through his film collection. Some were noir mysteries from the 40s, badly dated with their simple sets, stiff lines, deadly female leads and blaring musical impulses. Others were more modern fantasies, complete with bloody displays, facial distortions and personal terror.

Mulled through some of his favorites...*Psycho, Rear Window, Dial M For Murder,* transition efforts in the hands of Hitchcock, chuckling as he took viewers on those black/ white journeys that frightened, surprised, horrified.

He noted the lessons of *Double Indemnity*, a black and white film featuring men sporting short ties, high belts, hats and blousy trousers. A duplicitous woman lured a sniffing male into inescapable trouble. A killing hidden from the audience...quick strangulation, and what a payoff. Hard to overlook the warmth of murder wrapped in cash. But this black widow of a woman...appalling. His gut tightened. Women were despicable. All trash...all of them.

He compared those screenings of the 40's to the thriller, *Blood Simple,* shot forty years later. Black and white settings infused with color now...deep blacks, eye-soaking reds. Filled with the Coen brothers' imaginative camera angles and slow, deliberate narrative, the film affirmed Hitchcock's comment that it took a long, long time for a man to die.

A killer, M. Emmet Walsh, advanced the plot by postponing death until he expired while gazing into twisted piping underneath a wash basin. Its entangled curves and tubes...writhing, overlapping...became a graphic image of his last look on a complicated life now draining drop by drop. That caught Steve's attention. Is that what he had to look forward to? Bag man, hit man, dead man. Eh?

In its controlled flow of events. *Blood Simple* remained a film of personal dynamics which had no historic setting, one which could have occurred in any failed relationship, in any city. Tone, tempo, tune, all projected a taut, dark journey in the hands of actors whose work was as natural and convincing as licking a lip. Long silences created tensions and imaginings. Quite unlike, he thought, a different treatment of betrayal, *The Third Man.*

In stark black and white, Joseph Cotton and Orson Welles cast a steady tempo of energy, discovery, and betrayal in post-war Vienna. None of that in the Coens' work...nope, not at all. Gunshots sounded and felt like real explosions, with real holes, and real death. Got to credit the brothers for creating a new look into an old genre, he thought, one he could use.

And Francis McDormand, beautiful in her youth, but already carrying distinctive looks, remained convincing as a decisive killer. *Femme fatale.* Whew. Not as mischievously calculating as Barbara Stanwyck in *Double*

Indemnity, but unfaithful nonetheless. Were they role models for what his wife, Eleanor, was thinking? Would she betray him? Was she having an affair? If so, with whom? Needed to spend some more time on that idea.

He let his mind wander some more. Along came *SEVEN.* Shocked him and that didn't happen often. Judgment writ large, on film and in one's mind. Homicide shook the public, make uneasy the sleep of the innocent. Shockingly moral rituals condemned man's misbehavior. A menu for murder found in a catalogue of sin. Scary as hell. Serial murder...why and who might be next? Galvanized a community. A killer who became the object of everyone's attention. An unknown person who occupied everyone's thoughts. Powerful.

Serial homicide. The idea took over a very small part of his thinking, but it grew as he continued to drop the derringer back and forth, one palm to the other, pondering *Blood Simple* again, a femme fatale who ate at a man's desire to hold a privileged position in her life. Was Eleanor playing with him the way Abby played with Marty. Did he want his wife to continue toying with him or play the ultimate victory card? Eh?

More than one difficult dame had been disposed of as part of an apparently random but carefully calculated series of homicides that left her dead. Psychopathic meanderings befuddled police, amazed reporters, fixated the public, left them all edgy but curious. And here just seen, the *ZODIAC* killer proved *it could be done for no apparent purpose at all...and with different killing methods.* He took a deep breath, stood, pocketed the derringer. A lump of metal. His talisman. His tool. An 1866 pistol fit for a modern-day purpose.

He took a deep sigh, walked out of his screening room and looked around the living space. Trophy antlers on each wall. Rifles and shotguns racked under lock and key. Sliding glass frames protected a display of pistols and the dual derringers... collector's items, he thought with satisfaction. And over there, the bow and arrows that he used in fall hunting. A warrior's den, he thought, it was a place of action, a setting that could cradle a death plan.

He had needs...for excitement, for freedom, for release. Were his answers looming above and alongside him? Or was it just the thrill of homicide that moved him? Felt his stomach contract thinking about it. Hunting humans... he and them...cops and murder...marital release...police frustration. He could imagine newspaper speculations keeping the community on edge, cultivating the excitement of real life...and death. He could plot an intricate game of chase...lead the cops in a circle... arbitrary victims...no connection...mystify ol' Devlin...get to the final goal and then...release. Wealth would flow into his treasury and he would be free...at last.

He began shifting the derringer back and forth between his hands again...thinking.

RIVOLI

3

GESTATION

"Get over it!" Easy enough to say. Eleanor Gordon had run that slogan through her mind a thousand times, five thousand. More recently it surfaced with increased tempo, a little louder, a little more demanding. Every time she denied its command, she felt ill, a taste of bile trickling up to the back of her mouth. Pumping weights, work on the heavy sack, the staccato of the light bag, each task a little different, every rhythm distinctive, but the music remained the same. Steve, oh Steve...what have you become? Somewhere, somehow, what you showered on me in courtship, you abruptly removed upon our marriage. Was I simply a goal, a trophy, a reward for a successful courtship. And now, what are your plans, Steve? Let the poison seep out even as you smile, keeping me in your sights, offering me only calculated passion and jabbing verbal criticisms? Is that it? She grimaced.

But was she really a wounded dove? Had she been abused or had she put herself into jeopardy? If so, maybe it was her responsibility to get herself out...to restart her life...to escape.

What did Steve care about, really...hunting, money, movies...control. He video-taped his shooting sessions, counting bullet holes or analyzing his archery technique, sometimes pressuring her to try her hand with the compound bow. On occasion she would line up an arrow, draw it and watch the steel tip pierce that target. POP! Hmmph. Felt good. Seemed benign, hitting a bullseye, but it could be a deadly launch.

Truth be told, archery might have featured clean air and bright targets, a nice recreational activity, but Steve changed it into a blood lust sport...stuffed animals that leaked fake blood set up for targets. Ugh. That took it a step too far for her, but he laughed at her revulsion, ridiculed her posture, diminished her very existence, and when he was not concentrating on her, he turned his attention to other visuals.

Movies. Movies about death. Film stars caught up in attempts to bring reality to the ugliest of acts...murder. They fascinated him, kept him in the screening room for hours each week, sometimes spending more time there than he did at the gym. Mix those two preoccupations with his search for live game and it left little time for his real job...stocks, bonds, financial instruments of different kinds. He was a fading figure from the man that she married three years ago, increasingly a bulk that threatened to squash her, destroy her sense of self, keeping her a target for his verbal assaults. A psychological hunt? Was that it? Maybe at first, but he evolved.

A loving man when they wed, she learned soon enough that he needed control, needed to direct her attentions, judge her behavior, levy continuous review of her every move. He became short tempered, argumentative, accusatory, then dangerous. Stunned the first time he hit her, she had to build new skills...flattery, deflection, insincere praise...and consider the ultimate goal...escape. His professions of love always counter-balanced ferocious accusations of her behavior...her betrayal. She just didn't understand the pressures he dealt with...she didn't cook... she hated hunting...and she complained about money, the lack of it. She made him hit her, he said. It was her fault. And she could not respond to that...could not balance his demands with her survival. Best strategy was to stay away from him...let him follow her if he felt the need... work out separately at the gym, run long distances, be where he wasn't.

Divorce might give her a legal leg to hobble about, but would it protect her? Doubtful. The rage he vented in the privacy of their home would simply become a public embarrassment wherever they met...the gym, the movies, shopping, sipping coffee at Ole's. His mass was inescapable. She would continue to be an electron, orbiting, waiting for another force to split his atom... waiting. For what? Fate? Luck? How long could she wait? How long could she survive? Somehow, the nucleus had to be disturbed. It was very risky to force a collision, to become a free particle...but more dangerous not to. It was time. At least it was time to begin.

RIVOLI

4

RESTLESS

(Middle March)

Devlin turned, groaned, readjusted his body to the left, and propped up his right arm on the other pillow. A cramp moved into his calf and he straightened the leg gently, readjusted his shoulders and let his mind fall into neutral… instructed it to go back to sleep. Another minute and his breathing slowed, legs warmed and shifted slightly. His breathing became deeper. He fell back into his dreams.

He found himself walking slowly across a small field, being led by a scent he could not seem to escape. Ahead, guiding him as though attached by an invisible line to his belt, Jonas Kirk crept, nose up, eyes forward, an occasional caution to stay quiet. Devlin hushed himself, then found his mind in the air, hovering over Kirk as he unwound a cloth strip, revealing a clothed victim punctured with wounds, a pincushion of pins and knives grinding away with every roll. A victim. Someone Devlin knew. Startled, he returned to his body, yanked on the invisible line and shouted to Kirk, "Stop! For God's sake, stop...there's a body in there...it's ...stop! KIRK STOP!" He felt Kirk turn and reach for his arms, pin them to his side and look deeply into his eyes. For the first time, he spoke, "Easy, Devlin...easy...it's not what you think. I have it under control."

Devlin struggled against the grip, felt a panic begin to reach into his throat, wrestled some more, grabbed Kirk's coat and tried to throw him to the ground. "Dammit Kirk, this time I've got you, I'VE GOT YOU!"

"NO! YOU DON'T! DAMN IT, CHESTER!" Geraldine shouted now, "You've got ME...and now I'm wrapped up in the blankets...let go, damn it, LET GO!"

Devlin moved instantly through the curtain of sleep and...felt his arms around Geraldine's body, absorbed her kicks into his shins, heard her voice and knew instantly that there was no villain in sight. No Kirk. No fear. No sudden death. There was just Geraldine, talking now, "Jesus, Chester, you got me all wrapped up in these blankets again, screaming in my ear. Bad dreams are putting me at risk of being assaulted by a cop...and I don't mean in a good way. You awake, now, hon? You awake?"

"Hmmmmpphhffff. Yeah...yeah...not dreaming anymore...you O.K.? Didn't hurt you?"

"No, I'm fine, but I don't wanna be awake at some ungodly hour of the dark, Chester. You get your mind sorted out and get back to sleep. We'll talk some more in the morning."

"Hmmmph...whew...ya, o.k...yeah. I'll get back to sleep." He turned over to his right side, wrapped a blanket over and between his knees, propped up his left leg, wrestled himself into a relaxed posture, and let his mind wander back to the dark place, this time unoccupied, empty, a universe without stars. In less than a minute, he was breathing deeply again, sleep undisturbed 'til the dawn.

Geraldine felt his body grow warm, felt his chest rise and fall in a gentle rhythm. She adjusted herself and said once more what she had been telling him for the past couple of weeks. "Chester, you're gonna' have to talk to Kirk about whatever's on your mind...talk to him."

He was losing too much sleep of late, she thought. Good reason to turn off the phone and the alarm last night. He'd thank her in the morning. She slept.

He awakened late, near 7:00 a.m. Found he had rested well, stretched his body and got up. Used the bathroom, took a shower, popped a couple of pills for blood pressure, brushed his teeth and dressed. Walked slowly into the kitchen, stopped, attracted to the scent of coffee, the whisper of fried eggs, and the snap of a sausage finishing its dance with death, he thought. And there it was again... death... infiltrating his dreams, keeping him, a homicide detective, on edge day and night. Had to be a purpose to all of that. Poured his coffee, sat down at the table as Geraldine folded the eggs.

"Morning Mr. Butterfly...flitting about in your dreams and wrapping me up into a cocoon I don't wanna be in... feeling better this morning?"

"Eh, yeah, I guess. Slept pretty well...didn't like my dreams...sorry about screaming at you...had a problem I had to solve, somewhere there."

"You kept hollering at Kirk, not something that I object to, Chester, but I don't know what he has done to bother you so."

"Hmmmphh...not really sure myself, gonna' have to think about that, Maizie. Eggs ready?"

"Almost. Toast?"

"Yeah...wheat, buttered, with apricot jam, three slices."

He sipped more coffee while she finished preparing his food. Served it to him and left him with the morning paper, turned on the phone and went off to get herself ready for her day. He had the day off. He felt rested enough, whatever his dreams put him through, and he thought some more about Jonas Kirk. Why? Not sure, but lately he had begun to want to sort through their relationship a little more. No harm there. But his dreams seemed to caution him about getting too close to Kirk. Fair enough. Next time they had occasion to work together, he was gonna' look him over a little more carefully. Maybe then he could think less of Kirk and change his dreams back to those of Geraldine. Those usually worked out pretty well...he smiled.

The phone rang.

He parked toward the very back of the lot, backing into an empty slot, careful not to brush into the young saplings at the edge of the woods. He looked around, felt comfortable knowing they would end the evening there and privacy would protect their ritual.

They approached the Rivoli Theatre leaning into one another, joking, laughing lightly. He made a last comment to her and moved into the ticket line. She wandered over to the window display where the graphic for _The Third Man_ was projected in stark black and white shadows. Perfect, she thought, pondering for a moment how in the world Orson Welles could still command an audience so many years after his death. Well, here she was, and she was with her guy. He came over to her, mentioned again how important it was that they had this special time together. She loved hearing his whispers, recalled again how coincidental it seemed to be...to meet him here at *the first in this series, Murder Mysteries, that the Rivoli was sponsoring. Once a week. Couldn't make them all, but one a month...that was their plan...that they could do. Easy to arrange with her husband and children...mama just needed a night out, and hubby certainly wasn't going to spend an evening watching scratchy black and white images blaring stilted dialogue and making stark, stiff movements for 120 minutes of nonsense.*

She turned again as he handed her the tickets. It was a habit of theirs. He bought. She controlled. They entered the theatre, laughing at their mutual recognition of the little routine that they had created. Nothing but fun... popcorn, soft drinks and that special connection they enjoyed. Side by side, hands filled with goodies, they left the snack bar looking forward to the rest of the evening and a fuller, more complete resolution of the night. Finally, the lights came down and the music began, that Third Man Theme. They were transported into post-war Vienna replete with mystery and murder. Their night had begun.

Sgt. Oliver Grant sorted through the few cars left overnight in the lot next to the *Rivoli Theatre*. Felt relaxed enough having put down a couple of midnight cheeseburgers and a shake. Why would anyone go to the movies and not drive on home? Always amusing to him. Did they meet someone and to mutual surprise went elsewhere to finish the night, leaving a car behind them? Was that it? Maybe. He noted vaguely that this new murder mystery series seemed to have drawn a new audience to the theatre. March boredom? Parking lot filled. Older faces. Maybe.

He smiled. Maybe it was just mid-life needs finding late night seeds. Perhaps a need for imaginings flavored with the glistening black/white images projected in the simple language of noir film classics. Wondered what the menu would be two months from now. Once a week, just by driving by the marquee and through the parking lot, he could tell there was murder at the *Rivoli,* sometimes in the language of the staid images of the 40s, sometimes in the clipped, dialogue of the 80s, sometimes in the caustic portrayals of human flaws mixed with the gritty, grizzly intensities of death emerging from Hollywood in the last decade or two. Hoped the Coens' film, *Blood Simple* would show pretty soon. He'd make time to see it.

He wound his patrol car around the front edge of the lot, moved slowly to the street, glanced at the marquee and grunted with satisfaction, *The Third Man.* He had a nodding acquaintance with it, something about Joseph Cotton and Orson Welles, a 1940s black/white murder mystery. Alida Valli played the feminine lead, and he remembered thinking that she could have succeeded in *Casablanca* if Ingrid Bergman hadn't been available. Marvelous screen image.

He started smiling as he recollected other mystery faces of the era, images of Barbara Stanwick, Robert Mitchum, Fred McMurray and of course Humphrey Bogart. He always found the genre attractive in its succinct, almost blurted dialogue, the stiff posturing of its characters, followed by strained efforts to heighten drama with sudden bursts of music. Not much sexiness in the innocent stare of a femme fatale and the likelihood that she might indeed bring a new look to an old story: love entwined with murder.

He shook his head a little remembering Charlton Heston and Janet Leigh in *Touch of Evil*. Heston, an awkward Mexican official, Leigh a dynamic, pointy breasted woman being shuffled back and forth across the border as the plot ebbed and flowed. She could carry a murder mystery along just fine without becoming a victim as she did in *Psycho.* And then, Orson Welles...whew...power, force, huge screen image, spewing a bit of spittle over his fat lips, puffy face and huge cigar. Hell of a film.

He moved past the front of the theatre, paused at the other entrance to the parking lot and shone his spotlight around. Not much to see there, but, what the hell, nothing going on in Woodland Park on a cool, midnight morning and Devlin was off duty. He could just take a little time and mosey around back there...maybe park and let his 'burgers settle. He sighed, moved the car into the darkened spaces only recently abandoned by movie fans. Hmm. From this side of the lot he could see one other car that wasn't apparent with his initial drive by. Parked way in the back, it faced out to the lot, hidden from easy viewing, blending into the silhouette of a grove of trees on the adjoining property.

Peculiar. Maybe someone simply stashing their car 'til they could get help to get it towed home. Odd placement though. Still, nothing to really be concerned about. Maybe a couple of lovers trying to hide as best they could until they either awoke and fled or still inspired, tried again. Drove over a little closer.

Shone the spotlight directly on the grill, moved it slowly up over the hood, fixed it on the windshield... and saw nothing. Well, that was just a bit strange. Who parked a car in this out of the way place and left it? Lovers slumped, sleeping below the dashboard? Was that it? Maybe not lovers...maybe drunks. Smart enough to avoid driving, not smart enough to monitor their drinking. He smiled.

Grant drove quietly over to the sleepers. Nice enough car, he thought, a Honda. Appeared to be silver and relatively clean. Stopped, curiosity getting the best of him. After all, lovers or not, they might best be asked to skedaddle on home. He lit his torch, walked slowly up to the driver's side of the car, flashed the light inside and froze. Looked hard. Felt his gut contracting...once, twice...

then a fearsome writhing effort as it sent everything he had eaten at midnight supper hurling onto the ground, splashing the side of the car in its freefall, dotting his uniform leggings with particles of beef, staining his boots...ruining every effort he had put into looking professional...and he didn't care. Didn't care at all.

He stood there, resting his arms on the car, eyes shut, weight forward, mouth open and drooling, resting, gasping for clean air, gathering his senses. Finally, he stood up, wiped his mouth with his sleeve and took another look. Same as before. A woman, sitting upright in the driver's seat, headless. Amputation cast blood down her front, threw little drops against the windshield, the side window and doubtless different corners of the interior. Next to her...he looked hard...tilted a man deathly still, a small bullet hole in his forehead. WHAT THE HELL!

A jumble of thoughts began to form behind his mumbled oaths of dismay. Where was the head? Why decapitation? Other passenger not assisting defense of any kind? Shot first? And then, silly as it sounded even to his semi-organized mind, he thought...the *Third Man*... the killer. Was Welles roaming out of time? Had the Coen brothers created a new shock film. Was this Janet Leigh, or Frances McDormand? Maybe Barbara Stanwick sat there in front of him...cut off in mid-saucy remark. "Bullshit, Oliver," he spat it out, "This is no movie."

He called it in. Desk Sergeant Oswald booked the call at 4:39 a.m. Homicide, double homicide right there in Woodland Park. Never happened before. Well, he knew what to do next...hated to, but protocol...had to follow damned protocol. Picked up the phone, punched buttons and waited for the ringing to end in Devlin's growling voice. No answer. He must have needed sleep bad. Left a message. Well, Grant was on the scene and the Coroner was always on call. Dead people weren't going anywhere. He'd get ahold of Devlin in a couple of hours. No problem.

RIVOLI

6

SORTING THROUGH

Devlin tossed himself awake. Didn't like the feeling. Reached over to his bedside desk and turned on his cell. Messages? Yes. Before he could cue them up, the phone rang. Wrestled with wakefulness, finally answered it. "Yeah...who's this?"

"Oswald, Lieutenant...you awake?"

"No, Oswald, I'm talking in my sleep...what's up?'

"Got a homicide, back lot of the Rivoli."

"Well, Christ almighty...whose handling it?"

"Sgt. Grant. We want you on the scene right away. Coroner is waiting to give you first assessment of everything before he starts working to remove the bodies."

"Bodies? As in more than one, eh?"

"Fraid so, Lieutenant. Man and woman...one headless, the other sporting a hole in the head. A mess."

Devlin sighed. Really didn't want to drag his ass out of the house on this morning...a day of rest...to sort through body parts in a parking lot. Still, that was the job."

"O.K., Oswald. Gonna' get a quick bite here...be over directly. Thank the Coroner for waiting. I'll hurry."

He sat back for a moment. Maybe this would be a good opportunity to spend a little more time with Kirk. Might have a chance to assess him more closely...work with him on a homicide, start to finish. Yep, gonna' do it.

"Kirk here."

"I need you now!"

Pause. Kirk looked around his kitchen a bit, sorted through what he could of Devlin's voice, marveled at his tone, his declaration...that was novel, but o.k. with him.

"What's happening Devlin?"

"Murder, double homicide, Rivoli parking lot."

"You on the scene?"

"On my way over now. Meet you there...15 minutes?"

"Yep. I can do that. See ya."

He hung up, paused a moment, surprised. Why would Devlin summon him at the very beginning of a case? Maybe he was warming to him after these few years. He certainly wasn't impulsive. Well, it'd be fun to be right there at the beginning of a homicide investigation. Last time that happened...hmmm, well Emily Porter's death of course... guess that murder on the Empire Builder counted...and the killing of the biker...ah, yes, the bishop...mmmmm, maybe he had been at a murder scene more often than he thought...almost enough for someone to think that he had something to do with the victim's death. Well, this time he would be there at Devlin's invitation. That had to calm him, for sure.

Finished a deep sip of coffee. Great day for breezes and sun. Great day to be alive. Not a good day to die.

He saw the Coroner's wagon parked there in the back of the lot, a small group of men and women hanging around the outside of the yellow ribbon which created an arc 30 yards deep circling the car, continuing its path into the woods, marking the death trap. Devlin there? Yep, walking about in a small circle, head down, his crushed fedora still atop his head. Wonder if he had breakfast already...well, a glance at his shirt... Kirk smiled at that thought, ambled over. "Devlin," he spoke the name with some respect as he approached him, "What the hell is happening here?"

"That's what we're gonna' find out, Kirk. Coroner is ready to take a good look. We'll let him do his business and then we'll ask some questions and sweep the site."

"Fine with me. What do you know right now?"

"Called in about 4:30. Sgt. Oliver Grant. I was sleeping in, no duty today so my phone wasn't on till well after 7:00 a.m. That's all I know. Got any coffee with you?"

"I am not a travelling sippy cup, Devlin. Let's sit in your car 'til Coroner's done."

"Good."

Thirty minutes later, they got some answers.

"Well," Dr. Hanratty began, "It's a mess, that's for sure, but I can assure you that both are dead," he smiled. "There's some gunshot residue on the upper torso of the headless one...blood flow makes me think she was shot before cranial amputation and the bullet didn't leave her skull. It's out there...heading up our inquiries," he smiled. The other body...well, also shot, right between the eyes... must have been looking at the killer. Looks like a small caliber entry, but we won't know for sure until we pull it out of his head."

"Blood splatter?" Devlin asked. "Does it tell us anything at all?"

"Well," Hanratty looked at his hands as he talked, "It would appear, at first glance, that the driver, the woman, was sitting there, fully clothed, no hanky-panky going on... up until then anyway. Killer seemed to have walked up, opened door and fired into her head. When the passenger turned, he got his in the center of his head. Now, without the cranium of the driver this is really speculation, and I'm extremely curious as to why the victim's head is not there."

"And where it might be, eh?" Devlin asked.

"Yep, have your guys look around in the woods...might find a face staring back at them."

"O.K.," Devlin responded, "Got any ideas on when all this happened."

"Well, rigor is well set...gonna' speculate about 8-10 hours. Don't hold me to it."

"I will," Devlin smiled. "I'm gonna' go through their clothing and see if I can find any I.D. That O.K. with you?"

"Be my guest," Hanratty bowed a little and cast his hand toward the car.

Devlin motioned Kirk to come along with him, gave him gloves and gestured toward the bodies...you look through the woman's stuff and I'll go around and sift through the guy's clothing."

They both went to work, easily finding identification, a little loose change, ticket stubs, keys to residences, driver's licenses and a few family pictures for both. Kirk pulled out a small tape recorder and entered their findings for future reference.

"O.K., Devlin...the woman is Lisa Leslie, age 35, married to a Murray Leslie, and to judge from some of the pictures, she has three children, two boys and a girl. She is, or was, blonde, nicely composed face, pretty really, and she wore her hair cut short. Nice spring dress before it got dipped in blood draining from her head. Had a nice smile. Height recorded as 5' 8", weight about 140 pounds. What you got with the guy?"

"His name is Elliot Peterson, probably 6 ft tall, 190, slender. Brown hair, narrow face, and he was pretty good looking 12 hours ago. Dresses casually, but well."

"Any thoughts on blood splatter?"

"There's not a lot of it. Her head drained down her, but not much more to see I don't think. I'll let the M.E. people sort through. Should have a report in a day or two. Whaddya think Kirk?"

"I agree, Devlin. Killer walked up from the woods, opened driver's door, shot woman in face or head, then immediately shot the passenger who was turning to look at him. Then, and this is the weird part...the killer amputated the woman's head. Violent, vicious act... carries a lot of passion, anger...would seem to suggest jealousy and desperate rejection, eh? Maybe carrying out a long-time grudge? If so, some guy is pretty damn explosive."

"Yep. You figure that the shots would have been heard...just two, bang...bang?"

"Well if time of death was closer to midnight than 10 p.m., most people might be asleep. And our shootings are here near a movie theatre and a dense, unpopulated woods. Easy to just dismiss the noise if we're talking a small caliber pistol, and I think we are. But that is a self-defense weapon and our scene is clearly some kind of revenge murder scene. But anyway, yeah, if someone were wide awake, then they might have heard the noise."

"I'll have Oswald get some foot patrols down here and canvass the homes...not many, won't take long."

"Sounds good. Well, anything else to wrestle with for now?"

"I'm thinking not. I'll follow up with the search efforts and get any autopsy information and blood splatter reports. Back in touch with you in a week, maybe two."

"Sounds fine, Devlin. Glad to be of help. We're looking for a pretty strong killer, inflamed passions...got to be to lop off a victim's head. Maybe military background. Takes strength and frenzied commitment. You know that, right?"

"I do. But you know, a thin, strong tensile wire is pretty sharp. Hell, I'll bet Geraldine could do it if you pinched her butt. But if you think of anything weird, let me know, Kirk. That's your specialty, right," he smiled, "Weird".

Kirk looked back as he walked away, smirking, "I've been known to find it, Devlin...usually when you can't." He laughed, "Wait to hear from you."

He walked on without another backward glance, but he was interested in these deaths. The violence was so unusual. Be interesting to see how it all sorted itself out. And who the hell wanted to murder Lisa Leslie, anyway, 'cause she was clearly the target. Well, if she was with her lover, the list of suspects began with her husband. Poor Peterson...just collateral damage.

Still, he was dead.

RIVOLI

7

SURPRISE

Devlin rolled over again. One last time for the night, he thought. Long day yesterday. Easy enough to trace down Lisa Leslie's husband, Murray. He was right at home wondering why the hell she hadn't come home last night... angry that there no message on his cell. Had just hung up from a call into the station asking Oswald if anyone could take a look-see around town...maybe she was stranded for some reason. Devlin checked Murray Leslie's reactions very closely when he gave him the news. Almost fainted... then collapsed. Took him nearly ten minutes to gather his nerves enough to look Devlin in the face. Nothing guilty about this reaction, and Devlin began to regret that he had to share some details about Lisa's death.

It took him a little time, but he finally edged into the question that he knew would unravel a lot of the mystery about her death. "Mr. Leslie," he began finally. "Were you aware that your wife was found with a passenger who was apparently involved with her?"

Leslie looked away for a bit, brought his gaze back to Devlin, squinted his eyes, mentioned casually, "Oh sure. She was going to the movies with her brother, Elliot Peterson. They do that about once a month...both fans of the murder mysteries that play at the Rivoli. Is he O.K.?"

"Well crap," Devlin thought, "If Peterson is her brother, what is this going to do for my theory of a revenge killing of a wife by an angry, jealous husband. Out the door with it...damn."

"I'm sorry to report to you, Mr. Leslie, that Mr. Peterson is also dead, shot to death at the same time, in the same vehicle. This looks like an execution, your wife losing her head and all."

Devlin stopped. That wasn't very good phrasing at all. He cleared his throat and tried again.

"Ah, Mr. Leslie, the evidence at the scene would indicate that the murders were a product of some intense passion...anger...revenge perhaps, by someone known to your wife. My theory now is she was the intended victim, and Mr. Peterson was simply in the wrong place at the wrong time."

"My God! Why would anyone want to kill Lisa? She is...was...a good person. Cheerful. Loved our kids, put up with me, ran the house, had plans to get back into teaching when the youngest was off to college. She and her brother were close, so close...and had been all their lives. We all kid that if they weren't siblings, they would probably have made a good marriage...all in good humor."

"Homicide is a mysterious matter, Mr. Leslie. It really is. Often deeply personal and outrageously public at the same time. Sometimes, people have grudges, real or imagined, that lead to violence. One possibility is that somewhere in your wife's history, she made an enemy, or more likely from what you say, someone believed she was an enemy...and he decided to punish her...and did it in a most horrific, violent way."

"You say that is one possibility. There's another?"

"Well, yes," Devlin responded, "Always the chance that we are dealing with a psychopath...someone who gets a thrill out of murder. Everything in life is just dull, and he lives without conscience as we might know it. What appears to be a random act, can be the behavior of a very sick person satisfying a need to feel something."

"You think that is what we are dealing with here...my wife murdered by some psychopath?"

"Too early to say, Mr. Leslie. Give us a little time, and we'll see. In the meantime, it might be wise if you and your children were to take some time away from Woodland Park. Got anywhere that you could go?"

"Well, yes. Guess we could head on out to Colorado. Family in Estes Park. Pretty in the spring. Might do us good."

"Might indeed. We'll be keeping a close eye on your home until after services are complete and watch it while your away."

"There's nothing more for me to do?"

"No Mr. Leslie. Your challenge now is to absorb a terrible loss and find your way to a new balance in life. Same thing for your kids. They'll probably need some psychological support...maybe a family counsellor."

"I see..." Leslie's voice tailed off and he began to mentally drift into some other state of mind. Devlin saw his face readjust itself, saw him gather some energy, felt that he was going to be strong enough to carry this passage with the children.

Well, he muttered to himself, that was a hard conversation. Today, a new agenda. He eased out of bed, showered, letting soft water wash away some of the stink of yesterday's discoveries. Probably consult with the Coroner again and then get together with Sgt. Grant and go over the whole event one more time. Wonder if Kirk has any thoughts about this?

He sighed. Without a lover in the car, Lisa Leslie's death seemed completely random. No motive. No explanation.

Sad.

He scrubbed away more grit from yesterday's discovery, shaved, dressed and headed into the kitchen.

Geraldine, already awake, had coffee ready and the frying pan gently warmed.

"What's it gonna' be, Chester. Eggs, pancakes, maybe a waffle?"

"Pancakes, I think...thin like you make 'em...got any bacon?"

"I do"

"Four-five slices and then some toast. I'm still waking up, Maizie. You know seeing Murray Leslie yesterday, learning more about his wife...finding out that she was with her brother in a regular outing that they do about once a month...well that doesn't leave me much to go on."

"Find out anything about the weapon, Chester?"

"Small caliber, Coroner says. Probably a .22 pistol...no casings though, easy to conceal. Got to figure that Lisa Leslie was shot with the same weapon...just no head to prove it."

"Blood splatter?" she asked, as she sat the red bottle of ketchup alongside his plate. She still didn't like watching him mix it into his eggs, but what could she say. "Blood splatter?" she asked again.

"Oh, not much...her head drained when the killer lopped it off, but her heart had stopped already...just blood draining," Devlin mumbled, using his toast to shovel egg into his mouth. Didn't say another word. Shook out some more ketchup...kept eating. Finally took a break, looked around, "Couple more cakes, Maizie?"

"Of course, Chester. So what's your next step, see the Coroner?"

"I think so. I'm not sure what more he can tell me, but we'll talk. Then I think I'll have a little visit with Kirk. Maybe he has some ideas. Usually does. Sometimes too close to the truth to be a casual bystander. Never have understood that."

"Well, remember Chester, he doesn't really have anything else to do. It's not his profession...maybe just a passion."

"I guess. More coffee?"

"Right here...you finish up now. I'm off to shower and dress...having a nice luncheon planned with Sharon Cunningham. Haven't seen her in a few weeks."

"Good enough," Devlin replied, holding the coffee mug in his hand, staring into the black a bit, then to the walls.. "You be careful out there, Maizie," he cautioned as she left the room. She looked back at him, just smiled, her orange hair framing her face.

"Course I will, Chester. Love you."

"Me too."

Sighed. Sipped his coffee.

RIVOLI

8

WARM HEARTS

Kirk kept pedaling. Thinking. Puzzling. Humming lightly on his early morning ride to Twin Lakes. Open air might clear his mind, he thought, maybe inspire some sudden insight. He reviewed what he saw yesterday: remote parking space, sudden shootings, no struggles. One bullet to identify...good. No head popping up in any strange places. No indication of pre-planning, but the decapitation was not on impulse. Motivation? Devlin told him yesterday that Lisa Leslie was sharing the car, and the movie with her brother, Elliot Petersen. Not unusual said her husband, something they did from time to time...no schedule...and they shared an interest in murder mystery films.

Where exactly was he to go with this information? Maybe ask about footprints. Enough dirt on the asphalt to carry any or were they destroyed in the initial inspection of the car? Probably were. Really odd to have Lisa Leslie both shot and decapitated. Someone must have had deep anger, resentment, vengeance...something ugly...that he needed to take out on her. Or...he thought some more... or he needed to just kill...the act of a psychopath. Took some strength to lop the head off a body...not done with a machete or a knife...too clean for that...probably a wire. Ugh. Not a pretty thing to think about. Yet, it was probably the key to solving the murder. Two victims. One distinctive. The other a bystander. And then there was the killer...the third man...he gave a wry grin. The phrase was the title of the movie playing and it had something to say about the drama in the parking lot. Any connection? Well deception was the storyline in The Third Man. Maybe that was the message of the killings. A psychopath giving a clue through movie titles, through film plots?

Deception in The Third Man...deception in double homicide, eh? Who was the real victim...the woman with the lost head or the brother with a bullet in his? Or neither?

He looked some more at the lakes. Time to head back into town, to Ole's. Not gonna' get much more thinking done out here. Needed some sweets and coffee...maybe some conversation with Sharon Cunningham. He called her on his cell, got an answer.

"Good morning, Jonas," she practically purred.

"Yep, it is. I'm out here on the bike trail near Twin Lakes, Sharon. Ready to have an apple fritter and some coffee at Ole's. Want to join me?"

"Is this a date, Jonas?"

"Well," he smiled, "It's an appointment. Whether it flows over into a date depends upon what we share. You available?"

"I'll be there in about half an hour."

"I'll be biking right in."

"Mount up, Jonas," her voice smiled.

He liked that. "Rolling now," he answered and touched OFF. Plugged in his ear buds, tuned to the local radio station on his iPhone and headed on to Ole's. Music to his ears? Not yet. First voices were from "Mike and Roxie" chattering on about the news of the morning and the gossip floating around about it.

"So Rox, if I walk up to you and point a finger and say, "Bang, Bang," what'cha gonna' do? Fall down dead?

"I'm gonna' bend that finger over and let you shoot yourself where the sun doesn't shine, Mikie."

"What if you didn't see me coming...maybe I surprised you from around a corner...think I could get away with it?"

"You mean like the "movie killer" here in Woodland Park? Seems like the storyline in the film followed a happy couple out of the theatre into their car. Murder by a Third Man, eh?"

"Seems like it, Roxi. Can't seem to get away from this story. No killer arrested. No suspects being talked about. One day old and already seems like a dead end."

"Surely you jest."

"Tried to think what Orson Welles would do with a script like that, Roxie. Think he would find it believable?"

"I think that he would see himself as the killer, saliva dripping from his fat lips as he took out the whatever to lop off that woman's head. Losing one's head....old expression...new meaning, eh?"

"Well, if you want to be sure you don't lose yours, Rox, be sure to lay in a supply of ZBox remote finders. Attach them to items you might misplace and then find them with your iPhone app."

"Oh my. Oh my. My Mikie. Slipping in another commercial in the middle of a sad, sad story of sudden death. Have you no shame...no courtesy?"

"Just enough to let you know that our time is up for now, Rox. See you at the top of the hour...y'all stay tuned out there for a new morning feature, "How to Park Your Car.""

[Laughing] "It won't be on the air long, Mikie and don't forget, my sign off is Roxie Rochambeau...two names. It's in my contract."

"I won't forget Roxie. And out."

Kirk smiled as he pedaled. Those two made a morning seem as though it were the best part of any day. Roxie Rochambeau...long name, smart, terse dialogue...she amused him. Thoughts shifted.

Sharon Cunningham...an impulsive call to her and she is responding with warmth, invitation maybe. Can't seem to figure out what she is offering, flirtation or fancy. Well, last time he sent out a look she sent it right back, without comment.

He pulled up in front of Ole's, parked his bike, locked it and thought about taking the front wheel in with him. Decided not. Woodland Park had theft from time to time, but here in front of Ole's? Not likely. Went on in and there she was, toward the back, looking at him, eyes a little narrowed as though waiting for him to cross an invisible barrier and enter her lair...her web...her boudoir? He felt the signal all the way across the room, ignored it and went to the counter.

"Morning, Ole. Got some apple fritters and coffee for me?"

"Ya, Ya, you betcha, Jonas. Have a seat...I'll find ya."

He pointed toward a cinnamon bear claw, "Add that to my plate, will you Ole'?"

"Ya, ya, good choice, Jonas."

He turned away and walked with some caution back to where Sharon Cunningham sat, gazing a bit now at her coffee, using a stir stick to give her something to follow, letting her thoughts meander to their morning resting place. She felt his presence, looked up, "Good morning, Jonas."

He detected a new scent and it wasn't just sugared icing...it had a tinge of sage to it and a vanilla so slight that he could scarcely identify it. Might as well start there.

"That a new lotion you're wearing, Sharon?"

"It is. Imported from India. I think they called it Mai Taj. You find it notable, Jonas?"

"I do."

He sat, waited a moment while Ole' brought him his morning order, arranged the plate and cup so it reflected his sense of order. This might be the last thing he controlled in this conversation, he thought...might as well have it my way. He smiled.

"Well, I gotta say, absorbing your smile, scenting your perfume and my apple fritter takes me to some kind of heavenly treasure, Sharon," he smiled. "Good to see you. Been awhile."

"Well, you called me, Jonas. What's a girl going to do when her day is brightened by such a charming voice. Resistance seems futile, don't you think?"

Oh my, he thought. This is going somewhere and moving along a lot faster than I thought...gonna' slow it down while I enjoy my breakfast...then see if she is willing to pick up the pace again.

"Time out, Sharon," he smiled. I want to stay on this highway, but I need to spend a little time at a roadside rest."

"Why. The day seems bright and promising, so much more than an hour ago, don't you think?"

"I do...please store the mood and moment for a little time while I empty my head of any thoughts that would get in our way a little later."

She looked at him, saw an edge in his face that wasn't going away, just what she wanted to see...with that in mind, she would meander along with his thoughts, and then bring them back to her purpose...after all, what else was there to do on a lovely, sunny day?

"What's bothering you, Jonas?"

"Murder...actually two murders."

"You mean the *Third Man* horror show in the parking lot behind the theatre?"

"I do."

"Unusual here in Woodland Park, but not that rare... well, I guess if you include decapitation, it would be a more horrific statistic. Hmmm. So what have you learned...you and Devlin?"

"We know now that this was not a jealous husband avenging a cheating wife. She was with her brother. Husband knew about it...regular event for them...liked murder mystery movies."

"And..."

"And if we can't imagine or find an actual motive, we are left pretty short-handed in finding a killer...and clearly this is a rage-driven homicide...but why?"

"What about the brother? Maybe he was the target and she just got in the way?"

"We speculated about that, but you know her lost head tells us that she was the main victim...did a little workup on the brother...single, nice guy, no arrests, good job in tech, happy to share an evening with his sister."

"So, there is a dead-end, eh?" She smiled. Anything in regional reports to give you any thoughts?

"Nothing to get excited about...some anonymous assaults, a few unsolved robberies associated with violence."

"But no homicidal events that you could connect?"

"Nope...and I don't like that...need to find some kind of thread that would keep me looking for the next one."

Enough of this, she thought. She looked down at the floor near her seat, leaned over.

"Jonas, I seem to have a loose thread on the hem of my skirt. It's hard for me to see just where it is. The light is poor in here. Maybe we could go to your place and look for it?"

He paused. Looked at her directly and let his mind go racing a bit. Here she goes again...mood swings, reaching out to him, radiating heat. And the thought surfaced once more. What did Sharon Cunningham want? Dalliance? Courtship? Impulse expression? More to the point, he thought, what did he want from her, and to that question, he was more certain. Wasn't going to dilly-dally. Wanted her, more than he probably admitted, and it was a bright, loving day.

"I'd like that. Give me 10 minutes start. I'll bike home and the front door will be unlocked. I'll give your hemline a good look."

She smiled. Here we go. "Wonderful, Jonas. I'll see you very shortly...anything planned for the rest of your day?"

"I'm uncommitted, so far."

"Bye, Jonas."

He got up, walked to the door and headed on home. Put the bike away, freshened his face, and waited.

She arrived, driving slowly, beginning already the courtship of slow, sweet seduction. Paused after turning off the engine, fluffed her hair, got out and walked to the porch, adjusting her skirt as she went. At the front door, she heard a call, "It should be open...come on in."

She did...slowly...eased herself through the doorframe, closed the door and locked it with a quiet, decisive move. CLICK.

She turned back to him and without a word walked over and just pointed to the hem where the loose string was to be found, somehow...somewhere. He began looking and before he could find the edge, the skirt was on the floor and Sharon Cunningham was standing there before him without a thread below her waist, and before he could absorb that, she dropped her top and bra.

"It's lonely like this, Jonas. Let's see how our skin tones match up in the sunlight."

He matched her nudity, saw blended colors, shared deepening breaths. No mood for a hard floor.

"In here," he motioned to his bedroom. She nodded and they vanished from view. Lots to do, energy to burn, hunger to be fed.

There were no longer shadows when they emerged. He looked at her in dim light as they dressed. My God, she was so muscular through her smooth skin. Have to ask her about that. Thought about starting over one more time and then decided sex was not the answer he wanted just then.

"So, Sharon Cunningham, what does all this mean. Any carryover here?"

She reached down and stepped into her skirt. "I'm thinking that we are doing just fine the way we are. I'll find you. You signal me. We'll see how our moods intersect."

"No public appearances, eh?"

"Oh, no. I'm not really at that place in my life."

"Suits me. I'll keep my glances subtle and my invitations timely."

"And I'll keep going to the gym," she smiled. "Amazing how much stronger one can get from simple weight-lifting."

"And from bench pressing..."

"Jonas...you're turning my head."

"In what direction?"

"Well, one more power lift," and she dropped her skirt.

Damn, he thought. All this over a loose thread. Well, keep looking.

At moonrise, Sharon Cunningham left his home, left him in his bed, left him drained, content and happy. She smiled.

RIVOLI

9

COLD CASE

(Early May)

At first, it was just a few days. The official verdict sliced like a knife in Devlin's side. *Death by person or persons unknown.* The two victims, brother-sister, were buried side by side amidst a gathering of well over a hundred. Not a celebration of life, just a simple declaration of loss for Woodland Park, and it left mourners empty and afraid.

Take a breath, and it was a couple of weeks. A few more mystery movies nights and it was six weeks...and still no information that would help solve the murders of Lisa Leslie and Elliot Peterson. Devlin had called on the Coroner three separate times, to no result. His own cops covered the murder scene twice, carefully. A single .22 slug in Elliot Peterson. No casings. Blood analysis did not reveal any type other than that of the victims. No strange DNA at the scene.

Lots of unanswered questions, Devlin mussed, and the answers threatened everyone. Who knew what motivated the killer? Double murder? By whom. Why? Psychopath? No one safe. Who was next? Anyone? He became withdrawn, snapping a bit at Geraldine, grousing at everyone in sight at the station, sorting through evidence again and again...no direction there.

The *Gazette* reached the same conclusion. Published follow up photos of the crime scene. Ran a daily sidebar headline for a week asking simply:

KILLER...WHERE? DEVLIN SILENT? ARE WE SAFE?

What can the police tell us that they are keeping private? Why murder in a movie parking lot? Where's the head? Where's the killer? How much longer do we have to keep guessing? Eh, Devlin?

Not every set of eyes scanning the *Gazette* was alarmed. Steve Gordon's mood improved. His days settled into a degree of satisfaction. *Well, well, well. He had their attention and he could feel concern leaking out of the print into the entire community. And he controlled it. Satisfying. He savored the alarm.*

A few more weeks passed and as the social fabric remained unblemished, coffee-talk shifted targets. Fluttering moments of small crime...robbery, drunkenness, brawling...caught attention, but no new homicide disturbed the renewed, smooth surface now covering the community pond. Soon enough, the *Gazette* became silent on the issue and public gossip began to concentrate on whether the $500 Super Jackpot at Bingo was fixed.

But not everyone had lost interest.

Grant continued to make his patrols, rotating shifts that took him around town between midnight and six a.m. every third week. Quiet work after midnight. A little activity when the bars closed, but apart from a wandering drunk or a rare burglar alarm (almost always false), he spent hours and hours just letting his mind wander, capturing little thoughts that brought him back to the murders of Lisa Leslie and Elliot Peterson. Surely in his whole life the reality of these sudden deaths, their violence splayed out before his eyes, would never really leave his thoughts.

And as he mulled it over, he revisited the film playing that night: *The Third Man*. Nothing in it about severed heads, but a murderer did pop up out of nowhere, the third man, Orson Welles, who killed with diluted drugs, and escaped...well for a time. Just the way it happened in the parking lot. Chance? Had to be. But discovering that there was a "third man" and who that person was became the focal point of the movie. And here he was, doing much the same, wandering around a small town in Minnesota, wondering whether there was a killer drifting through streets looking for another victim.

He kept an eye on the weekly marquee as movies rolled in...*Rear Window, Psycho, Vertigo.* Hmmph. Powerful, scary and violent...much the same as the shooting in the parking lot. Well, *Sixth Sense* came and went, and he still felt safe enough...not part of the afterlife...yet.

He finally approached Devlin and asked if he could help sort through any clues that came in on the murders. He had an interest in homicide, Grant explained, and he was single. No limits on his time. Would like to help. No charge.

Devlin looked surprised. Didn't remember a patrolman wanting to work on his own time...to solve an apparently unsolvable murder, well two of them. Truth be told, the case was wearing him down. Almost like asking why the grass grew in a pasture. There was a reason...but it wasn't readily apparent. Needed to find the original root, the nutrients that both produced a stem and multiplied its stringers. Murder...where was the seed of the act? Still couldn't find a tangled web that might lead him to the first plant. Now, suddenly, here was Sgt. Oliver Grant asking to walk the pasture and look for subterranean networks. Why not?

Encouraged, Grant visited the murder scene again, walked about it as might a film director, hands framing it from different perspectives, trying to imagine the physical movements required if a killer could surprise a brother and sister sitting quietly in a car, talking. Kept looking at those woods. Noted the exit doors from the *Rivoli Theatre*, aligned them with the back lot, assessed the line of sight, kept a list of future mystery films that would be showing weekly. Looked it over carefully, kept it for reference. Some films he knew. The rest he bought from Amazon. Good daytime work. He took notes.

And while Grant sorted through Hollywood history and Bollywood incursions, Geraldine saw Devlin begin to slump as he worked his sources and kept coming up empty. The very first step in solving a homicide, apart from being sure when the victim died...was motive. Why was a perfectly fine human being sitting in a car, talking movie reviews with her brother, suddenly transformed into a piece of slumping flesh, mouthless now, and her companion silenced as well.

Geraldine could see the case wearing her man down. His appetite declined, not just for food, but for her. She took it personally, thought maybe she was letting some of the edges of her body become a little too relaxed. Finally decided to do something about it and brought the subject up while lunching with Sharon Cunningham. The *Tea Cup* was the right setting, quiet, small booths for private conversation.

"Damn it, Sharon...I just don't have a sense at all of what's botherin' Chester. Sure, I know the job is demanding and he has a great commitment to keeping the public safe...I'm willing to make all kinds of space for him to do that. But now, for God's sake, he's not really responding to my cues the way he did before. Sure, he knows I'm there...I can feel that he is depending on me... but this case is a terrible distraction...or else I no longer got it. Got any advice. I'm tired of giving it to myself."

"Hmmm. Well, Deeni, I'm certainly not going to sit here and tell you what's wandering through your man's mind, or his pants, but my experience with Father Lockhart proved to me that time blunts the edge of hunger, if you know what I mean?"

She looked at Geraldine to see if she understood. She did...nodded her head, listened for more.

"Yeah, yeah, sure, I know that, but I'm not talking about romantic seduction and wild gymnastics in the bedroom. I'm talking about simple, basic sexual drive, release. Hell, he used to look me over when I just walked from the sink to the kitchen table. Right now, his mind is elsewhere and so are his hands. Don't like it."

"Not going to doubt your analysis, Deeni, but I am going to offer you one thought."

"And it is..."

"Right now, you're feeling bad about yourself...not feeling very desirable, wondering if Chester's commitment to his job is taking time away from you...that maybe you are losing some of your own sexiness. It happens. If I recall, you gave me strong advice about my clerical explorations in India...told me to take the priest to bed and don't look back. I did. You also told me that time would dilute passion and then I could just take a powder. It did. I left."

"But when I got home, it took me many months to figure out whether I was still the entre' I thought I was. Finally decided that just because every shopper didn't want my packaging didn't mean I should be left on the shelf. So, I did something about it."

"Howd'ja figure that one out, Deeni? Hell, you look like a million licks today, and that was few years back."

"Well, I just began to work out...walk, jog a little...but mostly I began to put in time at the gym."

"The GYM! Holy Christ, Sharon, you working out at the gym...sweating, stinking, hurting muscles...for what? Did'ja get color coordinated outfits...a sports bra, what? Oh, hell! Never mind about that...better question...did it work?"

"It did."

"What...men came drooling?"

"No. But I decided that when they began looking, I'd be ready. Funny, once I created that mindset, I began getting invitations from new directions."

"So, racking your body with weights, ropes and gloves sent your sexual signals radiating out there, eh?"

"It worked for me...you don't know names, and I won't tell you...but there were a few, and then lately, Ahmed Hassan and I were quite happy for many months, and I think now I have a new secret to keep."

"What! I know almost everything that's goin' on around town, eh? Between me and Chester, we could write a book that would keep old maids snuggled under the covers for weeks at a time. So, who is it?"

"Can't say...but as Chester might respond, 'I'll get back to you on that'."

Geraldine took a good, long look across the table and saw what she needed to see...Sharon wasn't kidding... saw it in her eyes as they narrowed when she spoke about this new adventure. Well, Woodland Park was a small town. Wouldn't take long to find out who it is. She shifted subjects.

"So, the gym, eh. Something I should take up?"

I think it would give you something helpful to do... make you feel better, more confident...stronger too...if Chester couldn't see the results, you could simply throw him onto the bed."

Geraldine broke up with that line, laughingly said, "So, what's it cost?"

"Well, I pay $45 a lesson with my private instructor. Started me off very slowly and helped me gradually increase my reps. I'm a lot stronger now, healthier too, I think I can lift a lot with my hips," she smiled.

"My God, Sharon. You're talking dirty like you know what you're doing. It's all that good, eh...just working out in the gym?"

"It is. Of course, I give myself little tests from time to time...have one going on right now. Stamina is a wonderful thing for a woman, don't you believe?"

Geraldine sat quietly for a few moments...sipped on her tea, thought about ordering a new croissant...thought of Sharon's success in the gym. Decided to pass on the breads. A new way of life, she thought.

"O.K., Sharon. Who's your teacher? When do I sign up?"

"Raul. Just walk into *BodyMold* anytime, ask for him. Tell him I recommended him and get on his lesson plan. You'll feel better, and sometime soon so will Chester...and you'll meet some nice people in the gym. Surprise you to see who all is there."

"Sharon...if this works, I promise I'll never gossip about you again."

"Well, spread the word that you said that, Deeni," Sharon smiled. "Let's move on to the rest of our day, shall we. Go see Raul."

"Damn right! I'll bring that Chester to his knees," she laughed aloud, that joyous sound that sounded like a cross between a donkey's bray and a stuffed nose.

Sharon Cunningham walked into the outdoor air feeling surprisingly crisp, lively, full of energy. Behind her trod Geraldine, head up, smiling now, her eyes on fire, ready to target her physical revival, and corral her man again...lock him up between her legs. Well worth a gym membership. She brayed again.

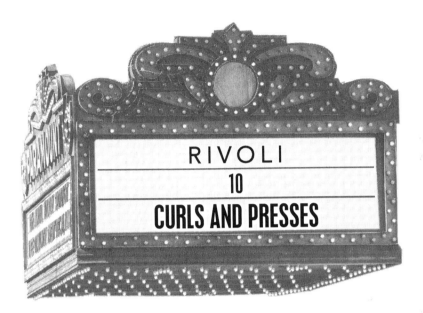

RIVOLI
10
CURLS AND PRESSES

(Late May)

Geraldine mulled it over. Gym? Hmmmm. Chester continued to worry. She fed him, cautioned patience with his case. Shared humorous stories of community foolishness until he smiled a bit and sent him off to work. Then she took a walk...a mile first, then two, then five. She visited about town, picking up gossip, spreading some, carefully reviewing business practices in tiny shops that felt immune to customer criticism. More than once, her loud observations had made news in the *Gazette*, and she felt a certain responsibility to be a good consumer neighbor.

But, as she began to feel more fit, she visited again Sharon Cunningham's idea of working out with a trainer, and one fine day she ended a mile walk in front of what would be her new daily destination, *BodyMold*. Even at first entrance, she felt herself undergoing a passage. A smiling young man at the desk welcomed her, asked about her interests, turned her over to Guido Mustakis, an absurdly fit fellow with a body so taut one could see little muscles moving under his skin-tight jersey. Geraldine was impressed, so much so that she forgot to ask for Raul. Well, no matter, she thought.

Guido walked her through the entire facility...weight room with both free weights and machines set up to make demands on lats, quads, biceps, triceps, buttocks and chest. A shadow boxing room featured a speed bag and heavy canvas punching weight. Running platforms offered opportunities to keep legs and lungs fit, he pointed out, then took her to a climbing wall complete with safety ropes. She rejected that challenge on the spot.

Smiling, Guido showed her a small pool for swimming and of course a complete shower/locker area designed for privacy and relaxation. A sauna invited tired bodies to take a few minutes and relax before finishing up the day with an invigorating, bracing shower.

"It is all here, ma'am," Guido said. "All you need to do is decide where you want to strengthen your body, and we will help you do it."

"I don't see very many people in here, Guido," Geraldine finally commented. "Are they hurt?"

"Ah, no ma'am, we are open all hours and we have dozens of our clients who spend their evenings here. Now, late morning, not so many, although you will see a few new faces every day."

"Well, I suppose if I'm gonna' start in something like this, I just need to take a breath and go, eh Guido?"

"That is the best way, ma'am."

"Well, let's start by your calling me Geraldine and my saying to you that I know that my hair is orange and that ain't gonna' change. Are we clear on that?"

"Ah...yes...Geraldine. And what are your goals?"

"Well, I like to walk...I'm sure as hell not a runner...but I would like to get stronger...whaddya call it, 'strengthen the core'?"

"Just so," Guido replied, "And the path to that is in the weight room...there we can start with very light resistance, build strenth and then improve your muscle mass"

"Muscle mass...you ain't thinkin' to turn me into some kind of freak are ya?"

"No, no, Geraldine," Guido smiled. "You will be strengthened but with the program I design you will remain smooth and molded, not protruding in any way."

"I don't see any women in here doing anything?"

"It is a slow time of the day, Geraldine, and a good time for you to begin...a private lesson would you say?"

She looked around some more. Saw a woman just walking into the room, going about her business adjusting weights on a bar under which she lay down on a bench and then proceeded to remove and lift the bar for three repetitions, rested, then three more...rested, then five more reps and she placed it back on its rack. Noticed two men in different sections, one pulling down some bar so that it rested behind his head, releasing, then repeating. The other was doing arm curls with weights in each hand, alternating. Neither paid her any attention.

"What they're doing, Guido. That's what I need to do... get stronger."

"I'll guide you, Geraldine," he replied with a smile, "And you will feel your progress."

She liked that idea. "Let's get started."

It took a couple of weeks, but she began to feel the difference in her torso, arms and legs. She nurtured

Chester, understood how stressful an unsolved murder could be for someone as conscientious as he was about his police work. She grew confident in being able to finish her workouts, could see that she was quietly accepted by others as a serious lifter.

Got great pleasure out of seeing her strength increase, then adding some weights and built up the reps again. Even took a little time to wander around the gym just seeing what other people were doing. Lot of activity at the wall climb, regular customers on the punching bags, speed and heavy. She finally felt confident enough to make quiet conversation with some of her training partners, especially two chatty women who liked to work out in the mornings. They fit nicely into Geraldine's comfort zone, gossiping and laughing, commenting on people who seemed to be very accomplished, some even a bit fanatical in their efforts. Name a few, she asked... and they did:

Walter Woods, insurance salesman who could float around the heavy bag and deliver devastating hits; *Isabell Dougherty,* known for her ability to scale the wall in 30 seconds; *Steve Gordon,* body builder with smooth, crunching muscles in his shoulders; *Ingrid Gresham,* outstanding at the bench press; *Dorothy Eisner,* fastest hands on the speed bag of any woman in the gym. They were all regulars, and Geraldine began to look forward to seeing these faces in her occasional afternoon workouts. Started with Walter Woods.

He was pounding on the heavy bag, working up a good sweat, focused on his left hook...WHAP! WHAP! POW, POW, WHAP! Whew, intimidating just to hear the sounds, she thought, wrapped her towel around her head to catch some sweat from her own set of curls, and spoke up to him as he paused.

"Say, there...I'm new, Geraldine's the name, and you look like you know all about boxing and striking...eh?"

Woods looked over at her, glanced up and down, decided to take a break. Took his own towel and wiped his face, hung it over his shoulders.

"Geraldine...quite a name for a petite little package, eh?" he smiled.

"Yeah...yeah. I've been called a lot of things, Walter Woods, but never 'petite'. You got an eye problem?"

He laughed. "Whoops, just a bit of my insurance patter, but you're not a customer-in-waiting, are you Geraldine?"

"Nah...I'm just here to tone up a little, put some strength in this lanky frame. But I see you here often... you got a goal in mind on that heavy bag?"

"I like hitting things."

"I see that. Must be frustrating trying to shake a tree full of people and find some who want insurance, eh?"

"It is. It's my job, and it's stress...still, I get to know people and sometimes one talk leads to another, and then to a new policy."

"I'm not interested."

"I picked up on that right away, Geraldine."

"So, whaddya know about these people I see here... any customers in your future?"

"Oh, damn, I never know...you don't mind if I swear a little?"

"Hell no."

"Good, good. Well, never know...strike up a conversation with someone one month, sell 'em a policy the next. Got a live one on the line right now."

"Names?"

"Oh, one of those women who are over in your area from time to time, Eleanor Gordon...might want some term insurance...I'll be visiting with her in the next few days, I guess. She and her husband, Steve, have taken out a significant amount of life insurance with me. Thoughtful, forward looking couple. Guess maybe she wants some more though she looks healthy as hell," he smiled. "Real healthy if you know what I mean."

"Don't squirrel around with that doubletalk stuff, Walter. Sexy lady and you like her a bit. Well, I don't see her often. She the one that spends time on the bench press?"

"Yep. She really works the curls and lats on the free weights. Supports her chest frame, you know," he smiled. "And she got interested in the heavy bag, so I showed her how to use gloves and position her body for a maximum power punch."

"I'll bet you did. She very strong?"

"Surprisingly so, but really quiet...just a hard worker."

"Well, maybe I'll get a chance to chat with her sometime."

"Just don't mention insurance...don't want her to be thinking I been talking too much. Her husband sort of lurks over everything she does too."

"Secret's safe with me, Walter. That heavy bag is sitting still now. Time to get back to it, eh?"

"Yeah, for sure. See you 'nother time, Geraldine."

She left the conversation feeling pretty good, more accepted. Decided to chat up some more of the regulars.

Reached out to Dorothy Eisner one morning as she finished her work on the speed bag.

Good choice. A little get acquainted chatter and then Geraldine began to ask about regulars. Eisner dove right into some quick assessments, made a few comments about various people in the gym, but once she got to Steve Gordon's wife, Eleanor, she could scarcely stop.

"Only see her when I work out in the evenings," Dorothy began, "But Eleanor Gordon's a maniac on the bench press...Ingrid says she puts her to shame even. Spends some time on the heavy bag with that Walter Woods and lately took up running...long distances. Must be training for something. I heard her talk about triathlons, but don't think she has done much swimming...can't do well in one of those with being able to swim well...really well."

"Heard her husband is pretty regular about his workouts too, eh?"

"Steve...that's her guy...ol' Stevie boy...yep, he's a regular here too...workout animal without any purpose, I think. Ex-military guy, a Ranger, Eleanor says. Doesn't talk much...sweats a lot...always here...works investment sales out of his home...shows up most any hour. Took up some kind of marital arts a few months ago. Likes to hunt too, according to Eleanor. She can't stand it...staring eyes in deer heads he mounts and posts on the wall...freezer full of venison...ugh. Can't even store ice cream in there... makes her sick to think about all those Bambi babies shot and butchered. When she complains about them, she says he just laughs at her. Says, 'Get a rifle and join the hunt.' Mean spirited fellow, but he doesn't say much of anything around here. I think she's afraid of him."

"Well, no wonder they work out at different times. Children?"

"None," Dorothy smiled a little wicked smirk, "Some gossip about Steven not being able to get closer than eight inches to her and that wasn't close enough."

"Not very nice, but is that accurate...to an inch?" Geraldine brayed and Dorothy roared.

"Well, any other news about them?"

"Oh, just that general stuff...she has nothing good to say about him. But I must say, and this is just for you, Geraldine, that insurance guy Walter Woods is here sometimes in the evening...saw him chatting Eleanor up a few times. I asked her about him, and she said he's just trying to sell her a policy, one she doesn't need, she says."

"Ohhh," Geraldine echoed. "You think he's an insurance man looking to score with a workout partner, eh?"

"Ahhh, I doubt it. That Eleanor is strong as a horse, yeah, but she's not the prettiest blossom on the tree. I'm sure Walter sees her as business, not pleasure."

"I'm sure," Geraldine responded, but she filed the information away with Woods' comments about Eleanor Gordon.

Apart from the gossip, Geraldine found Dorothy a workout inspiration...serious, regular and exhausting. She tried to emulate her, continued to build her strength and the reps. It made a difference. Still, while her body felt more alive than it had in years, she wasn't getting much of Chester's attention. His preoccupation with the unsolved double murder at the Rivoli Theatre consumed his energy, and he knew it.

"Maizie, I'm not much fun to be around these days, but I just can't seem to shake my anger about that murder. Worse, I don't have a clue and I'm not sure what more can be done. Gotta' be a motive. But what?"

"Chester, don't you worry 'bout me, darlin'. Curls and presses don't ruin girls and dresses. I'm havin' fun getting' stronger and when you get a clear mind, I think I'll be clearin' out a lot a' congestion in that body of yours, eh?"

"I'm lookin' forward, just not feelin' it right now."

"Relax a little, Chester. Somethin's gonna' happen soon enough, and shortly after, you're gonna' find yourself with a handful of smooth muscle that'll be completely new to you."

"You're a wonder, Maizie. I just need a clue."

Eleanor Gordon moaned as she rolled over, pulling a light blanket into a thick folded layer, placing it just under her lower back to support the muscles wanting to cramp. She touched her face, felt the swelling, wondered if the eye would blacken. Didn't move. Was she alone? Listened for sounds of Steve in the bathroom...in the kitchen. Silence. Was it safe?

Stifling a moan, she moved slowly out of the covers, slipped on a robe and padded quietly into the core of the house. Listened again...nothing. Checked the garage, saw the missing truck and relaxed. She was alone...for now. Went to the kitchen, set the coffee in motion and moved on to the shower. Let the water aim its little darts on parts of her body that didn't hurt, gradually shifted the shower head to her bruises, felt the warmth ease the aches, washed her hair, made sure the little scratches were soaped, twice. And as she cleansed her body, she began to focus more on purifying her mind. Where was her help?

It seemed like such a great match. Steve Gordon, famous local athlete, now a martial arts expert, successful stockbroker, bond trader, easy flow of income. She had her own successes in soccer and in volleyball...All-State twice in both. But she wanted to make a home, produce another generation in the image of her family's successes. She thought he did too, but like so many conversations uttered in courtship whispers, what she thought she heard, he did not utter.

He wanted nothing to do with children. Expected their marriage to provide a traditional balance, a 19th century model, she thought. He worked. She kept house. Sex as asked just part of it all. Romance not essential. And the routine they settled into within six months, seemed to become an electric fence that promised to last a lifetime. When she protested, they argued. A few months more, and they began a non-stop dialogue of differences. Now, when they fought, he hit her...slapped her really... and apologized instantly. But it happened again, and then again, and she knew her years were going to be a continuous nightmare. She reassessed.

He was a violent man. That was the reality. Surrounded with guns, knives, arrows, he became fascinated with martial arts. Devoted hours a week to the weight room. For what? Wanted to control everything around him. She looked at him more closely...a revelation. He was swelling up into a time bomb. Stuffed with certainties about all things, he pronounced irrevocable judgment on community issues, figures and policies...and dared the world or her, to contradict him. Dangerous. That's what he was...dangerous.

And his preoccupation with film...mystery movies, the array of DVD classics...bored her, absorbed him. He became transfixed with plots, made fun of foolish detectives, rejoiced in reciting their clueless mistakes. She noted with fear that he had slowly evolved into a person who challenged her very existence, who chose to control her just as he would direct making a film, commanding the behavior of cops and crooks.

Arrogant. Unending arrogance. Wonder what he thought about that double homicide outside the Rivoli? He came home from the gym that night full of himself, tension gone for a while at least. Smiling. Relaxed. Sorted through the freezer and brought out some moose meat to thaw for a pot roast. Next day, when he heard about the murders, he began offering her ideas on the causes. The killer? Could he solve it? She smiled. He now needed to share his superiority with the police...the world. Where would it stop?

Well, she thought, as the shower rinsed her hair. He had finally accomplished one thing...destroyed her resolve to stay in her marriage. Time to get away. Carefully. Slowly. She had a plan. Guess that was step one. Now for step two. Gotta get fit. Gonna' run...and run...and run.

RIVOLI

12

A DIM HAZE

(Early June)

He brought his small black bag out of the cabinet. Set it up on the kitchen table, zipped it open and looked inside. Plenty of pills, couple sacks of pot, half dozen folds of cocaine. Closed it. Time to head out to work, goods in his trunk. Would be going off shift in about nine hours. Nothing inside would spoil. He sighed. Then he smiled. Filling prescriptions based on need and cash gave him what he wanted in job satisfaction. This sideline made him a lot of fun money...all he needed really.

He walked into the **PRESX** building, a chain of small, personal drugstores begun in Wabasha, now covering most of Minnesota. His spindly frame slid unnoticeably through the doors, but his greeting to customers remained unfailingly warm and to fellow employees, correct and professional. Donned his white pharmacist jacket, his name, *Jeremy Wilcox, Pharmacist*, nicely aligned across his pocket. Looked about the store as though sighting a ship on a horizon, signed in for his shift and went to work. He hummed. A glance at his face revealed concentrated expertise. He smiled occasionally to customers waiting in line, but his faintly red hair, long chin and large blue eyes held their attention as much as his chatter might. He was a warm presence behind the counter, a pharmacist, a friend...precise, correct and pleasant.

Now in a large discount retail setting, he was one of a half-dozen professionals working hard long hours, struggling to keep their minds clear and the product pure and correctly filled. It was dynamic, but unprofitable really, and it was grueling.

The sick looked to you for relief, but they approached suspiciously, fearful that their meds might be restricted by insurance, worried that they could not provide the cash to purchase, concerned that their illness would get the better of them even as they put their faith in the bottle before them...tablets, liquids, pills, syrup...good for the day, or the week...maybe the month. It was not fun for him, dealing with the sick. Never saw a glance of appreciation.

Finally, he made the decision. He would trade assembly line pharmacy for the personal service of a small retail outlet, and he would find a way to make money flow in the right direction and in the right amount. Woodland Park fit his vocational need.

And his personal need brought him to *BodyMold* on a regular basis. Nice place to visit after his shift. Worked out with light weights, swam 30 laps in the pool, circulated through the gym, the sauna, the locker room, making easy conversation and subtle drug exchanges which calmed nerves and created new mental worlds. Cash flowed into his pockets. Customers poured into his private network, and he found balance, dual purposes: pleasing others, making money.

On this day, he finished up his shift, checked the paper for movies at the Rivoli Theatre. Murder mystery night, and he enjoyed the weekly look at old 1940's crime solvers mixed in with the much more sophisticated, recent expressions of human failure that sallied forth in support of an audience. Bought his ticket, popcorn, a large soda and took his usual seat toward the very rear of the theatre. Amused himself with the pre-feature quizzes, enjoyed the previews and settled in for the tense explorations of death in the film, _SEVEN_. A threatening film, it put him on edge. Dark, seemingly irrational murders stood revealed in layered complexity at the very end, just the way a mystery should.

Film over, he walked slowly to his car, nicely marked with darkened glass all around. He loved the look of the secretive motorist, one likely involved in something illicit, but not a clue in sight. He smiled, confident that his little cache of drugs was safe enough in the trunk of his car. Opened the door, noting somewhere in his mind that he thought he had locked it. Slid into the driver's seat, turned to grab his seat belt and hook it in place.

A quick motion blurred before his eyes and in a moment, he felt the belt around his neck, crossing behind his head to a balanced force that allowed leveraged hands fixed against the back of the headrest to draw the loop tighter and tighter. He struggled, flailed, tried to scream, lost breath, then consciousness. In five minutes, Jeremy Wilcox went from a pleasant, satisfied pharmacist to a slumping lump of flesh, locked in the black hole of his car. Once inert, he became a simple, manageable corpse, and the killer fired a .22 caliber bullet into his head, then looped the wire around his neck, swiftly pulled, see-sawed. So quickly done, Wilcox's head did not move. Killer smiled. Time to leave.

The parking lot emptied. The rear door of the Buick opened tentatively, then fully, and a figure slid out, carrying a head by its hair, moving quickly, athletically. Paused...picked up a box from just under and behind the car, circled over to the passenger door, opened it and set a frozen head on the seat, placed Jeremy Wilcox's head inside the box. Closed the door, quietly...a click...and moved swiftly into the woods. There, the dark sanctuary absorbed the killer and his new package. Jeremy Wilcox now boxed and sealed...and gone.

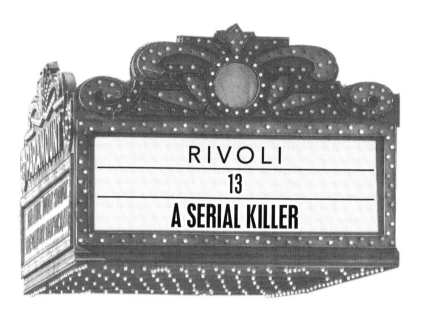

RIVOLI

13

A SERIAL KILLER

Sgt. Oliver Grant slept throughout the afternoon, arose near five and ate some steak and eggs. He read the *Gazette*, enjoyed the comics, did the crossword puzzle and took a look at the listings for the Rivoli Theatre. Mystery movie night again, and he had the evening off before going back on duty the next morning. Put his flashlight, gloves and some binoculars into his car, along with some rain gear just in case, and set out in what had become a ritual. Night off meant night patrol for him as he continued to puzzle out some kind of connection between the murders he stumbled across nearly three months ago and the movie of that night, *The Third Man*. Nothing to convince him yet that there was a link, but then again, nothing to say there wasn't.

He watched some early evening TV, got into his patrol car and made his way around Woodland Park. Scanned the Acres, visited the parking lots at the school, went by the bingo hall at St. Mark's...weekly fun there. Gave a look at the parking behind and around the Rivoli Theatre and noted the movie title. Always good to know what sort of thrills the patrons were experiencing. *SEVEN* blazed across the marquee. "Hmmmppphhh," Grant exhaled a bit. If ever there were a film that might link itself to human behavior it was this examination of the seven deadly habits...sloth, gluttony, greed and the like, all sins punished with murder. If there were some connection between that first double murder and the film, *The Third Man*, it might be expressed again this dark evening. He went through the parking lot slowly, finding bobbing heads, sheltered lovers, and late arrivals. Nothing to keep him from moving on to other edges of town. Visited the library, drove through the state park, making a few couples nervous, but again, nothing to hold his interest.

At midnight, he stopped at McDonalds, grabbed a quarter pounder and coffee. Clear, quiet night. Movies were for watching, lots of fun fantasizing, he thought. Not much good for warning the general public about murder though. Any link between his case and *The Third Man*? There *was* a third man at the scene of the double murders...the killer. But so what? No evidence of a connection. Nothing to keep him up at night anymore. He's been following the marquee listings for weeks, nosing around the theatre parking lot, and it was a waste of his time. Wrapped up his thoughts, slipped into his car and headed home.

On impulse, still grinding, he took one last turn through the lot at the Rivoli and looked about slowly, finally fixing his eyes on a car parked back next to the woods. His butt tightened...breath deepening. He gripped the wheel more tightly and advanced slowly, turning on his searchlight to scan the area. Nothing to be seen but the car, a dark sedan, maybe a Buick but hard to tell in that dimly lit corner of the asphalt. Stopped a good five yards away and looked it over again from the seat of his car. Was there someone, something in the dark. Single figure. Maybe not. He got out, scanned the area again with his flashlight and walked up to the window.

Just a glance, that's all, just a glance and he knew that he was again looking at homicide. Single person, male, slender, hard to identify...no head. He put on gloves, opened the door, looked across the front seat and there she was, Lisa Leslie. Her head, blonde, still so cold he could feel light currents of icy air moving about his brow.

Frozen...how long? Probably since the time of the last murders, a few months now. Could not help noting again the movie playing that night. *SEVEN* featured a severed head as an expression of a psychotic killer's sense of justice. Scary on film. Repulsive in the flesh. He backed away and controlled his growing nausea. Didn't vomit this time. Couldn't decide if that was his growing maturation as a crimefighter or a sad reflection on his loss of innocence. No matter. He called it in.

Oswald confirmed the log time, 1:23 a.m. "Gonna' call Devlin right now," he said. Grant signed off on that.

Wondered how fast he would get here...didn't matter really. He was gonna' stay 'til they had sorted this out a bit. And he would think some more. Movies always had a cast of characters, some important, some mere distraction. What was he seeing tonight? A single victim unaccompanied, a severed head from one murder traded in on a fresh skull from this one...directly linked to the first set of murders. No longer coincidence. No longer random homicides. They were part of a reality film, the ugly remnants of choice. Question was why?

A serial killer was now operating in Woodland Park. Motive? Now that would be a challenge. Most of these psycho guys didn't really have a purpose...just liked the thrill of the kill...they would always be the main character. What about the supporting cast? Oswald reviewed it quickly: a brother-sister who apparently had no enemies and whose death produced nothing of value for anyone. That was it.

Wait, no! That wasn't it. He was part of this movie as was Devlin, even Kirk. After tonight, there would be more faces...unknown actors, maybe credited performers. Gotta' be more here than just a killer satisfying fantasies. Gonna' be some interplay between main character and these bit players. Heck. If all went well, some of them might become co-stars. Someone had to solve this series of killings...might be him. More likely Devlin and his expertise...but who knew. At this point all he had was an "other actors" by-line.

Gonna' need some plot direction, some emergent details about a series of homicides. Probably gonna' get some once this mess tonight hits the Gazette tomorrow... or the next day. More information needed. Maybe mass chatter will spin off some clues...need someone in the director's chair. Gonna' take some time...and thought.

He looked up, caught by the headlights turning into the lot, rolling silently but quickly, parking next to his patrol car. Saw a couple of heads inside...they looked the area over from where they were parked. Finally, the door opened and out stepped Devlin from behind the wheel and, to Grant's surprise, Jonas Kirk emerged from the other door.

Devlin looked over to Grant. Motioned him out of the car, introduced him to Kirk.

"So, what brought you out here tonight, Grant. Working overtime?"

"No, Lieutenant. Working on my own...told you I just wanted to keep grinding away on that double murder. Had an idea that I wanted to pursue. Think now that maybe I might be on the right track. But it's all a surprise to me tonight. Just about to head on home when I took one more look out here...and found this Buick here in the dark. First look inside told me I needed to leave it alone 'til you were here. I think we have some links we can explore."

"Fine. Let's take a look inside and then we'll talk some more. Brought Kirk along 'cause he has a smart mouth and sometimes clicks on the right answers. Seems to be a specialty of his."

"Heard a lot about you, Jonas Kirk. Glad to have you on scene."

"Well, Officer Grant, if you have a theory about these murders, you're one big step ahead of me. Looking forward to tossing ideas around with you after we take a look at the scene. And please call me 'Jonas' or 'Kirk'... makes me feel welcome and Devlin doesn't always do that for me."

"And I'll be Oliver, eh?"

"Done. Well, Devlin, shall we," and he motioned over to the murder scene. Maybe this time, they would find some evidence. Could always use some evidence.

Illuminated by a bright moon, they walked slowly toward the Buick, three exclamation points merging into a single silhouette.

RIVOLI
14
DEEPLY PERSONAL

She awoke near 5:00 a.m., checked to see if Steve were stirring over in his bed. He was not. Probably got in well after midnight. She reached over to her clothing rack, quietly picked up her short pants and jersey, slipped into her running shoes and moved silently out of the bedroom into the kitchen. Dressed and finished her cup of coffee in tandem with the last spoonful of yogurt and fruit. Nodded once to herself. Filled her water bottle. Plucked her iPhone from her fanny pack. Checked traffic reports. No disruptions. Put the phone away, quietly opened the back door, closed it tenderly and walked into the yard.

There, lodged in the ink, starlight offered reference points to guide the comets...and her run. She stared, surveying the silhouettes of budding foliage seemingly supporting segments of sky. Looking around, glancing back at the house, she took a deep breath and exhaled strongly. Steve was still asleep, the weight of his emotional eruptions stilled by a loose loop of heavy breathing, and she, now physically fit, could step out of his lasso and head to the open range. She took the first steps, walking nearly 50 yards, then broke into a light jog. How far today? How many miles? What would be a suitable release? When could she someday jog to freedom? Not yet. Not this trip, but she was getting closer. How many miles? Let's try 15, she thought, and increased her stride, keeping it loose and relaxed. Yep. She could make it. By the time she got home, he'd be gone and she could enjoy her space, embrace its true function...sanctuary.

He awoke struggling to hide from bright light, moved a hand, shielded his eyes with a corner of a blanket and sighed. Enough? Felt his body begin to serve his need... everything working, muscles tuned. Sore from yesterday's workout, even that one after the session at the gym, he smiled. Felt relaxed. Looked over to see if Eleanor were still asleep. Bed empty, covers folded back...listened carefully...house quietly enveloped him...freedom.

He arose, yawned, stretched, got into the shower and dressed in his loose gym clothes, fresh from the dryer. Ate a small breakfast...eggs and toast...and looked about the house. Tried it on for size...his home. Was it his? Parts, maybe. Liked the look of the three mounted heads: deer, elk and moose. Let his eye wander through the large living room...furniture all wood, strong presentation, a defined design in his dark blue carpet, lamps at key placements... all comfortable. Let his mind go into the movie room, began to run through his inventory: spy adventure, dark murder mysteries, wartime romance...all of them part of his viewing imagination...loved the action, the edge, the death on both sides of the law. Needed to buy some more and settle in for a nice viewing session soon. Thought about supper. Went out to the back porch and opened the *chest freezer. Plenty of menu here. Chose venison chops and set them thawing in the sink.*

Enough, he thought. Brought his lightweight, loose martial arts uniform out of the dresser, pressed and clean as he liked to keep it...Eleanor never put an iron on anything, he thought. Would exchange it for the heavier, used one in the gym. Liked to stay tidy. Today was going to be a real challenge. Planned to take on the heavy bag. Might lay back for some bench press work afterwards. Just depended on how he felt. He sighed. By the time he got home, the venison would be ready to cook...and Eleanor would probably be back from wherever she was, likely just in time to ruin the evening.

Sighed again. Maybe they could talk later today... maybe he could start a conversation a little more calmly. Would she accept it or go crazy bazooka the way she did the last time he mentioned her disappearing act. Good reminder right there of why he needed to know more about what she was doing. They needed to talk. She needed to explain...a lot.

Daylight illuminated Eleanor's face as she slowed her pace, returning home well sweated, worn down but not exhausted. Showered, dressed in a loose blouse and lightweight skirt. Looked about the kitchen for food...saw meat thawing. Gave it a good look...who knew what all he kept in that freezer: venison, bear, maybe slabs of moose. He kept chiding her to take up bow and arrow hunting if she didn't like the sounds of rifles. But she didn't like having anything to do with killing game. Someday, she'd have to sort through his stored meats and see what creatures he had harvested to fill a freezer chest, to put antlers on the wall. What was that all about anyway. Reclaiming manhood? Maintaining Ranger training? Well, Steve was looking forward to a good meal, one he'd cook himself, she thought. Guess that was all he needed to set out: meat with veggies in the fridge and bread in the drawers. Cave man menu.

Late afternoon. She grimaced. Heard his Ram extended cab arrive. The growl of the diesel interacted with the sounds of its tires crushing gravel...ominous, dangerous. The door shut with a firm clunk, not loud, and no cursing. Wondered why he spent so much time in that four-door beast. Dominate even traffic? Was that it?

She liked her Yaris.

He entered the house quietly, ignored her, went over to the thawed venison chops and inspected them. Seasoned two of them, returned rest to fridge. Placed the chops on the stove top bar-b-que and glanced over at her, eyes calm. Maybe they could talk.

She sat down in the divan, a goblet of wine in hand, glancing briefly at the moose head on the wall, its glass eyes fixed on her, its horns threatening to scoop her up. She took a deep breath, gathered herself enough to tuck her skirt under her legs. Keeping her eyes on Steve, she sipped once, then again. Set the wine down.

"Good day Steve?"

"I'm thinkin', yeah, so far."

"How about last night...catch a movie, what? Sleep well? You looked a little tense yesterday."

"Yep, new mystery at the Rivoli...*SEVEN*...good one. You heard of it? Got me on edge...those cops... so stupid and the killer...seems to just be out there, in the black... taunting them...whew...you should see it...really scary, but left me relaxed once I saw what it was all about."

"Hmmmm, doesn't sound appealing. What was it... seven guys hanging out together, shooting deer? Eh?"

He just looked at her, took in her body posture, didn't look as though she wanted to fight, but if so, he was ready. Was that how she saw him? Guys shooting deer for fun and talk? Took the chops off the grill. Grabbed some sauce, sat down, sampled them...more seasoning, poured some bottled blood on them and began chomping...to good effect.

"You seem pretty calm, Steve. Anything you want to talk about?"

"About the film?"

"No, Steve, about us, dammit."

There she went again, swearing, demanding attention, forcing conversation about them...again.

He waited, finished up the last chop. "Well, yeah, Eleanor, there is. Been thinking a lot...guess I need to get this off my chest...I'll start if that's what you want, eh?"

She tried to keep her tone civil, "Of course, Steve, what's bothering you? Something seems to be keeping you more edgy that usual. Having a hard time with the bond market?"

"Nope, Eleanor. No problem with the markets."

He wiped his mouth clean of the red smears. "This is all about you...gone...spending your days running. Escaping really, right? Disappearing for hours, sometimes a day or two. What the hell is going on?"

She looked at him, remained calm. He was so explosive lately, more than ever. Maybe let him direct the conversation.

"You cared?"

"Well, hell yes, I care. You're my wife. People see where you go. They learn things I don't know. Your putting me out of the loop. I don't like it...don't know what you're doing, where you're going. Sure I care. You're my wife, damnit.

She paused for a long moment, then gently continued.

"What did we get ourselves into, Steve? That we should end up here...scarcely willing to look at one another... how did we get here?"

"Christ, I don't know, Eleanor...but here we are...you, sniggling away from view, running to who knows where, scheduling your days to avoid mine...our life is just a series of gradual, growing silences...for months now. Our sex life is non-existent."

"No big mystery there, Steve. You hound me with questions, leave me with silence...work out at the gym until even the walls recognize your sweat. Slapped me around a few times. And you ask, 'What is it?' Well, I'll tell you what it is, Steve," her voice rose. "It's you...with your steady line of judgments, demands for loyalty, pawing for sex...really Steve, what in the hell do you think you are doing? We've been going downhill for well over a year. What's that all about?" She paused for breath. Resumed more calmly, "There's nothing going on in your life I want to be a part of, Steve. Nothing. You must see that."

Silence.

He wrestled with his words.

"Lots of questions pop up when you don't talk to me, Eleanor. I'm a stranger living all by myself. What do you think that feels like? Sure, I want you in my bed. That doesn't happen. You're ignoring me...smart ass remarks, insulting my hobbies, my life really...know what...you make me want to punish you for that kind of abuse. I don't want to...but you push me to it."

She hesitated, felt the urge to raise her voice, caught herself, thought a moment, then began, calmly, "I'm afraid of you, Steve...look around... what do I see...dead animal heads hung on a wall, a side room full of pistols, rifles and shotguns, longbows...a glass case full of an assortment of enshrined collectibles...derringers, Colts, crossbows, poisoned short arrows, long arrows... and worst of all, a freezer full of dead animal meat. Why this preoccupation with violence, Steve?"

"Hunting is a man's privilege, Eleanor, but you're welcome to join anytime."

"Not me. My God, Stever, look at your movie room... nothing Bambi-like in there, not a musical, not a dramatic film. I see nothing but video games simulating calculated murder, DVDs full of murder mysteries, frenzied violent martial arts...all of it a part of your comfort zone. It scares me... I feel you becoming more tense, more explosive. Right now, we're speaking...more than we have in weeks, and I'm still not sure what the point of the talk is."

He looked at her, face reddening, puffing, "The point is I don't know what the hell's going on in your life. You've changed...where are you? Who are you?"

Her voice gentled, "I'm right here, Steve, and I'm trying to find some stability. You scare me. You're not the guy I married...and I suppose that I'm not the woman you wed...but this distancing...it's getting wider, and it doesn't seem to be something that we can manage indefinitely."

Silence.

Finally, he broke the moment, "How the hell we gonna' ever deal with it when all I see is you running into the distance, pounding weights in the gym, firming up...and I ask, for who? I'm really not in your life. Who ya' grooming it all up for, Eleanor, eh?"

Pause.

She looked about the room, licked her lips, shut her eyes briefly, gathered herself. "I'm doing it for me, Steve, just for me. I want some control over my life. You earn a fortune trading stock, hedging bonds on-line. I earn virtually nothing, spend what you give me, fit into your life as you place me. I have no protection for my future. You tell me we have a large life insurance policy. I signed it two years ago, and I have to go to you to read the terms.

She paused for breath...looked at him dead straight, "My God Steve, *I just don't want to do this anymore.* Fitness is something I can control...keeps me a reasonable distance from your temper, makes me feel good about myself."

"And when you feel good, you ignore me more than ever. Really pisses me off, Eleanor. Think about it. You're really just a bit of mist in my life...fading, forming, disappearing to where, for what, with who?"

She stared at him. He locked eyes with her, his face puffed up and reddening, then he slammed his fist into the back of the large chair facing her...sent it flying across the room.

She didn't back away one step, "And when I am here, Steve, I feel like a third arm attached on your side. Useless but always there to be tossed about or tied in place, at your pleasure. I don't want that anymore."

He looked at her intently, his face filled with color, thought briefly of her remark, dismissed it, pressed his own storyline.

"You're having an affair...I can tell. Who is it, Eleanor?"

"Steve, look at me...seriously, look at me."

He did, his eyes now narrowed into slits, his face tightening, arms flexing in place.

"I'm looking. What?"

"I'm not screwing anyone, you jerk! Now, I'm not thinking that I want to live with you but for now, I have nowhere to go, no love waiting to greet me, no haven to shelter me, not even a cash reserve to feed me. I want out, but I'm not sure how to do that. So, I'm going to try running, lifting, thinking, and doing the best I can to figure out what's next. Right now, I'm just not sure."

"*Right now*," he made fun of her phrase, "Right now, Eleanor, I am sure...that you're going nowhere...run all you want, but you'll come home eventually, and I'll be here waiting for you. I'm not interested in changing anything. So, I'm saying to you, deal with it as you wish...just don't give me reason to find you out...'cause I will and then you'll give me no choice. And remember, even when you think you're running alone, I could be out there, in the woods, watching...and waiting, eh?"

She set her wine glass down. Gazed at it for a few moments, didn't look up, then quietly, with the speed of a serpent's strike, she spat, "*You're a pig*, Steve. I'm gonna' live my life. When I know what I want, I'll let you know." She looked up, held up the wine glass and gently tipped it in his direction...repeated, *"I'll let you know."*

There was a long pause, a newly discovered quiet that touched the walls and sharpened the space between them. Eleanor's wine glass needed filling. She glanced at the bottle of Cab...empty...and she remembered not at all how that came to be. Steven's bottle of bourbon was nearly drained. His eyes remained focused on her, inflamed looks promising more violence for the smallest misstep. Better to end this conversation. She said nothing more, arose, went to the guest bedroom, quietly closed the door behind her.

She inhaled as deeply as she could...caught her breath. Would it never end...and if it did, how would it end? She knew what he threatened...he'd slapped her about more than once, threatened to do it again...and did. The emotional terror was becoming intolerable. She looked at her hands...shaking, felt her gut turning. There had to be a way out...some way out. Had to be. She had an idea... just need to find the right moment. Timing.

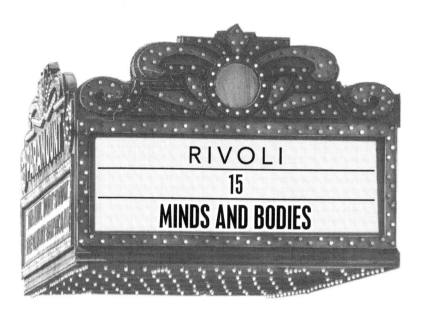

RIVOLI

15

MINDS AND BODIES

True to his nature, Devlin gradually separated himself from Kirk and Grant, cautioned them with a hand to remain behind as he slowly approached the driver's side window. Looked hard at the interior. Just as Grant reported. A white male, maybe mid-30s, headless. And there, Devlin could scarcely believe it, but there on the passenger seat was the severed head of Lisa Leslie. Almost perky, it faced forward, an unsmiling, but presenting presence, asking for respect, begging for examination. And she would have it, Devlin thought.

He turned to Kirk and Grant, motioned them to open the other doors and take a good look. "Don't touch that severed head until the Coroner has had his look," he reminded them, and then they quietly began to look for evidence. Body still in rigor, but they worked around it, Kirk looking through the back seat, Grant taking a careful review of the passenger side, commenting, "I can smell gunshot residue. Car keys on the floor"

Not much to see working with flashlights, but one thing seemed certain. His decapitated head had been exchanged for that of Lisa Leslie's, hers cold, his simply missing.

They decided to order some delivered coffee, sit and sip 'til it was daylight. Did not expect the Coroner 'til then anyway.

Slowly, the world brightened, soft rays of morning sun caressing them in ways that Mr. Dead in the car would never feel again. Devlin answered his cell, grunted "O.K." and turned, "Coroner is on the way."

Half-hour later, they got the doc's all-clear.

"O.K., Devlin growled, "Let's find out who this guy is and have another look."

Took a while, but first guess was that he had been dead for about eight hours give or take. Rigor still in control, but this time, Devlin wrestled through the clothing enough to haul out a wallet...took a look. "Some guy named Jerry Wilcox...got a Pharmacist ID card. Drugs is my first thought. Either of you know him?"

Grant and Kirk nodded "no" simultaneously. Devlin nodded again to the rear of the car. "Let's have a look inside the trunk."

Grant picked up the fallen keys and opened the back lid. Slowly. Kirk, stood waiting there, took a look, reported, "Got a small bag here. Come take a look, Devlin."

He did...unzipped it and stepped back. "Well, Christ, so this is what Mr. Wilcox is up to...carrying drugs around, selling no doubt. Got a stash of cash in here, so he must have finished his rounds for the evening...some scattered unsold packets, probably coke, syringes, a few pods of pot...guess it was a pretty good night for him...until it wasn't."

"Kirk, look through the backseat area now that we have some light. See anything?"

"Some threads of cloth, maybe cotton, clinging to the floor carpet and same fibers around the edges of the headrest. Not much blood flow. I'm just gonna' guess that the killer knelt here, looped something around Wilcox's neck and pulled...hard. There isn't much blood flow. May have caused his death by strangulation, or just immobilized him enough for a close-range head shot... maybe like that one we think he put into Lisa Leslie. Heart had to be stopped when he lost his head. Had to be a hell of a surprise, 'cause he doesn't seem to have tussled about much. You'll need some tweezers and collection vials, but this fiber might tell us something."

"O.K. Good. I'll get a post-mortem report in a day or two, and in the meantime, we'll go through this clothing closely, and that bag...remnants of drugs. Maybe some information in there about his rounds. Grant, you take control of it and sort through."

"And *moi*, Devlin. Do you have a task for me?"

"Well, Kirk, you tell me often about how you have thoughts, that you like to just sit and think about homicide... likely motive, probable killer, path to conviction. So, why don't you do what you do so well. Just think."

I took his words to heart. Truth was, I had no official placement in this investigation...couldn't really handle evidence, or anything that might tie our victim to a killer, but I could think about it, and I could take some time to talk about it to someone who had a lot of insight into the world of subtle criminality...Sharon Cunningham.

"I'll do it, Devlin. You and Oliver have at it. We can chat about it sometime soon. One thing I want to follow up is this guy, Wilcox's drug customers. Woodland Park isn't so large that I can't sort through some gossip and rumor and find information...might help."

"Suit yourself, Kirk...get lucky and learn something we can use."

Kirk nodded agreement, commented, "Well, one thing we can start with is the nature of these homicides here in the movie house parking lot."

Devlin paused, "What do you mean, 'the nature of these homicides', eh?"

"This is a serial killer at work, Devlin, no doubt about that. We have to focus on motivation, on behavior, and on a pattern that we might discover...cause it's gonna" happen again."

"I think Kirk is onto something," Grant murmured, "I've been toying in my mind with the listings of various movies that have been playing each week and those that are here the nights of these murders."

"You saying there's a connection between movies and homicide" Devlin asked?

"I'm still sorting it out a bit, Lieutenant, but, yes, if I were writing a headline for the *Gazette* tomorrow, I'd call them the *Marquee Murders*. There may be some plot lines in these films the killer wanted to call to our attention. Serial homicides usually have something linking them, fantasy, thrills, engorged cleverness, challenges of evasion. Maybe our killer wants us to be thinking about film plots even as his victims lie dead in the parking lot. Sometimes, serial killers want the game to be about making us look like dunces as much as they want the thrill of the kill. I don't know. I just keep mulling it over."

"Well, keep it all in mind, Grant. Right now, we're still on the loose for a motive. Nothing to connect Lisa Leslie to drug dealing, but the two murders are connected. Both featured gunshots we think, but they both included decapitation."

Then he turned to Kirk. "Whaddya' thinking about all of this movie stuff, Kirk."

"I like the flavor of it, Devlin. Oliver here has an itch for detail. Both sets of killings happened in this parking lot...a mystery movie playing...did it give any clues to plot lines and murder? If not, maybe we're not looking closely enough."

Devlin paused, drew a breath, held it...exhaled. Shwwooooo! "O.K. let's just work it that way. I'll watch over the Coroner. Grant, you stay sensitive to the marquee and evidence. Kirk, you find out what you can about Wilcox's customers, wherever they are. Then we'll talk. Now, get outta here. Sgt. Grant and I have work to do here. "Official stuff, you know," Devlin smiled.

"Right you are, Devlin," Kirk smiled, "Stay stout."

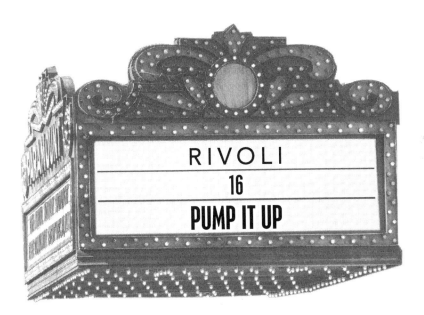

RIVOLI
16
PUMP IT UP

(Late June)

Geraldine walked briskly into the gym, smiling at the title on the entry: <u>BodyMold</u>. Well, she thought, not so sure that my body is reforming itself, but it is certainly stronger, and feeling far more agile and capable than it was a month ago. Chester seemed to like what he was seeing, and since he got called out on that second murder, he was a lot more relaxed. Gave him a new set of forensics, a new set of thoughts, a serial killer. He was better in bed, but he had a-ways to go. She smiled.

Checking in at the desk, she picked up her locker key, wandered into the changing room and converted the loud colors draping her body into a tightly fitted, green and yellow set of leggings and jersey. Swept tendrils of her hair back and under the bright pink head band that contrasted nicely, she thought, with her orange hair. Drew a breath and settled into work mode. Still didn't like a sport bra but had to admit it gave her a better range of motion, increased her performance. Wandered into the free weight room to see who was around today. Late morning usually brought some of the women into their workouts, and the chatter kept her agile and busy. Saw Ingrid Gresham working on the bench press, finishing up her set and waited 'til she found some breath and started right in.

"So, Ingrid, you setting any personal records?"

"Christ, Geraldine, been doing this so long I may have reached my peak. Don't want to bust a vessel or tear a muscle, but I'm thinking I could take it up another 10 pounds or so."

"Better you, than me, Ingrid. I used to think that I could just keep pushin' my body forever, but then I ran up against pulled muscles and some torsion twist in my back. Had to back off," Geraldine laughed, "Next thing I thought was maybe I should call ol' Walter Woods and get a life insurance policy. Wouldn't want my man, Chester, to have to pay to bury me"

"Say, Geraldine, that's a thought. My husband and I are beginning to talk about life insurance. Only in our '40s, but I asked my lawyer, Roger Blaisdell, what he thought about us buying a policy."

"What'd he say?"

"Oh, he said "You don't need one, Ingrid." Then he paused a long time, kept me hanging, then said, "If you think you'll never die."

Geraldine laughed a loud bellow followed by a nasal bit of squeezed, strained laughter. A bray really. Couldn't dismiss that insight, but still, didn't want to start dredging up future calamities.

"Damn downer bit of advice, don't you think?"

"Well, lawyers aren't known to lead a client into a romance novel...guess we'll all need a will someday... maybe some insurance along the way, too. I talked it over with Grover, and we decided to do both. Gonna' meet with Woods this week and sit down with Roger next week to write our will. Guess taking out legal papers on living is sort of a serious business."

Geraldine absorbed the idea, commented, "So, how much is he recommending, this Walter Woods?"

"He said at our age, we should just take out a joint policy insuring both of us for about $500,000 each. We're young enough so the premiums won't be too large, and if one of us dies early, well, the other has plenty of money to make the transition to whatever."

Geraldine absorbed the conversation, the amount, the conclusion and let it run through her mind. Chester was middle-aged and she was only a couple of years behind him. Lots of time to go, but hell, after that Rubber Ducky near death experience a couple of years ago, who knew how much time one had left. She'd have to take it up with him when he was under less pressure. And Roger Blaisdell...she'd heard of him all right, after his work with Chester on the *PumpkinFest* murders. He was a careful investigator...seemed to have a smooth way with the language, something she lacked, but appreciated in others. Maybe she'd just visit with him and follow Ingrid's lead. Information, calculation, execution. That might do it.

Well, enough chat she thought, time to work the body, and she set out to do her rotations. Sweat, groans, pain, and sighs. That's what it took these days.

An hour later, Geraldine finished up with some time in the sauna, then a gradual cool down swim...just a few laps, just paddling, keeping her orange hair out of the chlorine. Showered and dressed, letting the red, yellow and green dress wrap make her into a gift package. What next? Time to eat.

She parked her pink Cadillac a few spaces down from the front of Ole's, locked it up and swept herself into the café, letting the bell on the door announce her arrival. People looked, saw the orange hair and went right back to their meals. Rarely did someone ask her to sit and talk, knowing that anything disparaging they might utter about anyone would be spread without conscience as soon as Geraldine left the shop.

"Hey, Deeni," Sharon Cunningham called out, "Come on over."

She smiled at the invitation, felt a lot more relaxed and maneuvered through filled chairs and food-laden tables, carefully keeping her eyes on her destination, ignoring those close, shielded looks she could feel following her across the room. She felt resentments, but she murmured to herself, "What the hell...fill your faces and find something else to do with your lives...just do it right." That was all she wanted really, for people to do things the right way...her way.

"Sharon, what the hell you doin' in here at mid-day. Thought you spent this time at *BodyMold*. Figured that was why I haven't run into you much. Still challenging weights and reps, eh?"

Sharon smiled, "Well, Deeni, I've had some changes in my life, I guess...haven't given up pushing weights, but I'm using flesh and blood, not iron...and don't you ask me who. When I'm ready I'll let you know."

"You are being too cruel, Sharon Cunningham! I sit with you through bingo. I tolerate your affair with that Sikh, Ahmed Hassan, and see you flirting around with some of those local businessmen and you won't even let me inside the boudoir, so to speak, eh?"

"Oh, I'm sort of at an in-between stage in this latest love adventure, Deeni. Being swept away in the bedroom doesn't mean I want to have my name locked up in gossip. I'm having a good time teaching myself to be patient."

"And your guy...how's he doin' with this anonymity... bet he's married and loves it, eh?"

"Noted and filed, Deeni, but I'm not commenting. Now, what are you doing here, looking fresh from the gym."

"Hungry. Worked up an appetite in there pushing weight, swimming, just letting the sweat pour out of my body. Also picked up some gossip tidbits."

"Gossip you say?"

Geraldine smiled. "Trade ya."

"I'll say no for now...but what can you tell me?"

"Oh, really just a little talk with Ingrid Gresham while she was working out...guess she and her husband, Grover, are gonna' be buying some life insurance...you have some?"

"Well, I didn't think I needed any, but Walter Woods pointed out that I might. Don't care much about the life insurance part, but I have some destinations in mind for my estate, and he said a good policy would enhance the value of any distribution that I might set up in my will."

"Whaddya think of him...Woods...trust him?"

"Oh, I think I do, but I learned a long time ago, in India...she smiled...not to trust people to carry through on their patter...just be sure to read the fine print...so I will. But in general, yes, I find Walter direct and thorough and he seems to have struck up a nice relationship with Roger Blaisdell. I really came to admire Roger during that *PumpkinFest* crisis last year. A black man in this white community who simply goes about his business, building trust, speaking the language of a professional and laughing a lot. He has a great sense of humor, but he clearly gets serious about the law...really like him."

"Just how good is he at his personal interactions, Sharon. Anything I should know about his bedtime stories?"

"Isn't it delicious, Deeni, how curiosity can just become a consuming mindset," Sharon laughed. "I know nothing about his bed. He married a woman whose mother once lived in Woodland Park. Likes it here. Has kids. She's thinking about resuming law practice when they are a little older. I'm coming to learn something about his way of thinking."

"What? Anything special I should file away, just in case I see him cavorting around town a bit."

"Well, he looks for core solutions to problems and then finds ways to flesh them out. He was really important in tracing down the paperwork that convicted Jerry Fields, thank God."

"So, a kind of legal detective, would you say?"

"That would be fair, I think. I don't know for sure where Chester is on solving those movie murders, but if he wants some detail work done...some research...Roger could be invaluable."

"I'll pass that along, Sharon. Chester's getting a lot more involved in the job and less worrisome about what he doesn't know. Seems to be working pretty closely with Jonas Kirk and keeps mentioning this new Sergeant Oliver Grant. Don't know for sure what lines they are pursuing, but they've been keeping in close touch. Not sure which one of them has any real expertise in sorting through legal or financial paperwork, but Roger might be great at it. I'll ask Chester."

Sharon Cunningham looked up, smiled, "Deeni, you do that, and I'll try and sort out my love life long enough to be able to tell you something about it. Now eat."

Geraldine smiled, held up her hand, and hollered, "Ole' bring me a fritter, damn it! How long do I have to wait for service around here?"

"Right away, Geraldine...little coffee too?"

"Yep, sure, what the hell. Time to rev the ol' body up a little."

"Have fun with that, Deeni," Sharon said, as she rose to leave. "I'll keep an eye out for you at the gym...some of those women are grinders aren't they?"

"Yeah, they are, and that one guy, Steve Gordon, he's an animal with the weights...strongest guy there I have no doubt. I'd like to chat him up someday, but right now, I'm a little scared of him."

"Fear is the precursor to failure, Deeni," Sharon smiled. "Go for it. Find anything fun, let me know."

"And then we can trade professional gossip secrets, eh?"

"Well, we might well do that" Sharon laughed as she moved away.

Geraldine waved goodbye, sat there, nibbling at her food, thinking about what she could learn from Steve Gordon, wondering more about who Sharon Cunningham was bedding.

(Early July)

Oliver Grant shed his belt, locked up his gun, changed his clothing to casual civilian garb...khaki pants, plaid shirt, tennis shoes...and wandered over to Ole's. Ordered some Danish, a couple of iced cake doughnuts and sat nursing his coffee. What has it been now, a little over three months since finding the dual murders in the lot behind the *Rivoli Theatre*. Another month since Wilcox lost his head. He smiled a little with some satisfaction, knowing that he had moved a little closer into Devlin's confidence, enjoying the camaraderie of working with Kirk and wondering what exactly he might be able to dredge out of some linkage between classic movie mysteries and the reality of three homicides.

He started over again. *The Third* Man presented a plot that could only be satisfied by the existence of a killer not known to the police...the third man. It also dealt with greed, the theft of a life-saving drug that the victim had been diluting and selling on the black market. People died from the drug that was supposed to save them. In sum, Grant thought, the film presented a conundrum for the killer's friend. Ignore justice or be a part of executing it. How might that connect to the double murder in the Rivoli parking lot? Were Lisa Leslie and her brother involved somehow in black market activities? Was there a link between them and Jerry Wilcox.? Was it greed? Wilcox was selling black market drugs. Lisa Leslie's head, lopped off, ended up in the seat next to Wilcox, his own skull gone as though in trade. A message? Was this the connection to the second murder, a reason why it occurred when the film, *SEVEN*, was being shown.

He paused and found some strength in this scenario. *SEVEN* followed the trail of a vengeful killer who punished persons abusing the seven deadly sins: lust, gluttony, greed, sloth, wrath, envy, pride. But the sin most visibly punished, the one that no audience member could walk away from untouched, was the severed head, a punishment for greed. Well, Grant thought, he had a wandering head mystery of his own to solve. He had evidence of greed in the criminal behavior of Jerry Wilcox. He had a major plot line of greed in *The Third Man.* What he needed to do was find some connection between Lisa Leslie and Jerry Wilcox. Needed to do some more background work... well, maybe he could find an investigator, someone who could sort through legal documents, drug receipts, illegal movements of cash. He'd ask around.

Heard the door open and then Ole's voice holler out, "Hi ya Jonas...and a good morning to ya!"

"Right back at you, Ole! Got a fresh apple fritter in there somewhere...coffee to go with it." Looking around, he saw Grant sitting toward the back. "Bring it to Oliver's table...I'm gonna' chat him up a bit, eh?"

"Right away, Jonas."

Grant motioned him over with an expansive arm sweep. Good chance to sort out some of Kirk's thinking... wonder what he thinks of this idea of a movie link?

"Good morning, Jonas," he greeted, giving Kirk a few moments to arrange his food, take a bite, have a sip of coffee. Then, he gathered his thoughts.

"I'm sitting here thinking about movies and severed heads," he smiled, "and I'm wondering where to go from there."

Kirk shook his head slightly, "Well, Oliver, you're way ahead of me on this. I'm planning to wander over to *BodyMold* a little later in the day, but I haven't chatted anyone up over there...not yet. Not really sure what I may be looking for, or what I'll find, but I'm sure of one thing. Lottsa' bodies will be looking stronger than I am. How you doin' with the film connection?"

"Well, I have some theories, but what I need is someone who can go through documents, investigate files, find a paper trail and make sense of it."

"Hmmm. Whattya got in mind?"

"I'm just at a stage when I need some paperwork on the list of mystery films scheduled for showing. How long ago were they booked? Who makes the decision? Any changes in the original plans that might coincide with murder? And I'm interested in drug distribution. Is there a little local network that is moving money and prescriptions around for illegal profits?"

"Good questions, Oliver. What about life insurance policies? Who wrote 'em, for how much, when, for who? How many people do we have Walter Woods contacting? What if some of them have a drug connection? What if the whole homicide pattern is dependent on some insurance connection?"

"I think you're on the right track, there too, Jonas. If films are being arranged by anyone outside the theatre, timing to fit a murder, there has to be a motive for that... unless we have a psychotic killer who just likes to get his thrills from murder...and laughing at the cops."

"And we might."

"Yeah, a serial killer...and that would really put us in a fix...cause what we might think is a pattern might simply be the erratic behavior of someone pursuing a plot that is off our rational radar."

"Well, Oliver, to come back to your interest in an investigator, I have a name."

"Eh? Well, great...who?"

"Fellow by name of Roger Blaisdell. Local attorney fresh out of law school...worked with him on the *PumpkinFest* murders and found him to be highly competent, lighthearted, serious minded. He can get the job done for you."

"Think Devlin would hire him for me...help him get search warrants?"

"Oh, I think he would. I'm sure that his forensic work is leaving him with some questions too...and he knows Blaisdell, likes him. See what Devlin would like to do."

"I will. You goin' over to the gym?"

"Yeah. Plan to see Devlin first. Maybe find out a little about what he's thinking. Poke him into getting us together sometime soon and see how we can put all of this together."

"Good! Had enough of this sitting and sipping, Jonas. Let's get outta here and see what we can find out."

They rose together, wound their way to the counter. Kirk offered to pay, Grant refused, and they each slipped Ole a couple of bills to cover snacks and sips. Out the door they went, Alphonse and Gaston, making way for one another as they left the shop.

Kirk felt confident in the relationship he and Oliver were building. Nice to work with someone who spent time on thoughts as well as projected legal angles. Devlin was great at action. He really did like arresting people. Just needed some direction. Well, he'd go over and see what he thought about things...and Oliver's ideas for Blaisdell.

He walked. Took note again of the Acres...space, trees, shrubs, a haven for sitting and thinking and a field of play for kids...uncoached kids...kids having fun. Gave a quiet nod to St. Mark's parish church, again becoming mindful of some of the challenges of faith and folly that occurred in its pews. Brought Sharon Cunningham to mind again. Hmmm. Wondered just where they were going to end up, lonely singles looking again on the dating landscape... becoming quiet silent partners for the long term...or a publicly recognized pair who ended up being invited to various social events, approached for favors, asked to work a homicide or two. Well, who knew? Probably Sharon, and she would let him know when she felt like it.

Finally, the police station. He walked up the stairs, entered, nodded hello to Oswald and hollered for Devlin.

"Yo, is there a Lieutenant here who knows anything?"

Devlin looked up, closed the file on his desk, leaned back a bit in his chair and let out a quiet burp.

"Kirk! In here. 'Bout time we had some talk."

"You said you'd call us together again...time moving on...you got anything?"

"Come in, close the door."

Kirk settled into the guest chair, kept his eyes on Devlin's face, tried to read it, saw a bit of perky optimism. Hmmm. What now?

Devlin closed his eyes, moved his chair from side to side, digesting information, sorting through ideas, looked up as though surprised to see Kirk across from him. Began.

"I've had some new information back from the Coroner. Not sure exactly what it tells us, but it does help us build some theories I guess."

"Theories I like, Devlin. But I like real evidence even better."

"As do I, Kirk, but you take what you get. Here's what I got."

First, our local Pharmacist had a nice cache of stolen drugs in the trunk of his car. Nothing in his home. None in his system, so he wasn't a user.

Second, absence of large blood flow tells us that he was likely strangled by a belt, a cloth belt of some kind to judge from the fibers found around the head rest he was pinned to. Then he was likely shot, finally decapitated.

Third, there were fibers on the floor of the back seat, caught up in the fabric of the carpet and these fibers were also cloth, a heavy kind of fiber...maybe the stuff found in athletic garb.

Fourth, the head on the passenger seat still quite cold, so it has been sitting in someone's freezer since the first Rivoli murders. Whose?

Fifth, there was a ticket stub in his pocket, so we know he attended the movie...believe the title was SEVEN. Don't know anything about it...just that it was playing.

Sixth, the killer had great strength. Never could get too up close and personal with that headrest in between his hands, and after he shot him, it was hard to get a good angle with the wire to take the head off. But...and this is the important part...he did. Whoever did this was one strong stranger.

Seventh, found a folder in the glove compartment containing files relating to life insurance policies. Unsigned. Wilcox couldn't leave much to anyone without those documents signed and filed. But did the killer know they were not executed? Eh?

Eight, found nothing by way of DNA, blood samples, not even fingerprints on the door. Scratches on the lock suggest killer got in with a pick tool, used gloves, got out without leaving a trace. No footsteps traceable from around the car.

"So that's it, Kirk. I'm sleeping a little better 'cause I have something to grind on but no results...no fun banging up against the same wall. You?

"Nada. I'm heading over to the gym in the next few days...see what I can pick up...main thing to see is whether there are muscles on people that seem unusually large, unusually powerful...something they can build with the help of a pharmacist."

"Makes sense," Devlin muttered.

Kirk squinted at nothing, continued, "Then again, even thin people need a pill or two just to keep their stamina at elevated levels, let them be able to come back to their workouts without extended rest. If there's a drug connection in these murders, that's the place we ought to find it...that's my thought. Eh?"

"Would certainly help to put some flesh on the bones," Devlin perked up.

"Well, there's more. I was chatting with Oliver Grant a while over at Ole's. He's doing a nice job of thinking through the movie angle...think we should keep after that, and he could use some help...suggested Roger Blaisdell. You think you could make him legit and give him some warrants to do some searching at the theatre... records, bookings and the like?"

"Well, sure. Anything else need department approvals?"

"Well, yes. Again, Oliver would like to look into the insurance policy in Wilcox's glove box. Written but unsigned. He also thinks that Walter Woods may be circulating insurance policies in the gymnasium that might brush up against some drug users. Maybe a connection to Wilcox. Eh?"

"Hell yes. Let's turn him loose and let him see what he can find. You got anything yet?"

"Nope. Gonna' circulate over at *BodyMold* sometime this week. See what I can dredge up by way of gossip and see just how any of it might fit into what Oliver is putting together."

"O.K. Good. I'm beginning to feel like we're closer to working a normal case, Kirk. Just have to grind down on potential motives and see if it can lead us to what is turning out to be a powerful, motivated and ruthless killer."

"Well, yeah, but don't forget, Devlin, we might be in the midst of some psycho whose motivation is a secret to us, something buried deeply in his own mind and experience. If that's the case, normal evidence just leads in circles... not much satisfaction in that."

"Might make a movie in itself, eh," Devlin grinned. "Maybe I can get a bit part for Geraldine. She's getting really interested and she does gossip."

"No argument there, Devlin. Give her a hello for me. I might visit with her and see what she's picking up in the word mill over there at *BodyMold.*"

"Well," Devlin laughed, "If it's gossip you want to gather, my Maizie's the one to talk to."

"Maizie?" Kirk looked curious.

"Oh," Devlin looked a little sheepish. "My name for her."

"I think that's sweet, Devlin...quite unlike you."

"Leave, Kirk. Go do something useful."

"I'm on my way, Dad."

"Damm it...get outta here."

And he did.

RIVOLI

18

SWEATING, MOANING

I'd put it off long as I could. Walking into a sweaty, loud workout space clanging with weights being dropped or max reps being tested...well...it really wasn't what I wanted to be doing with my day. But, I'd promised both Grant and Devlin to sort through some customers, and there might be something to be found here.

Saw no one in particular. No sign of Geraldine or Sharon. Looked at some of the other bodies in various postures and decided I'd just pretend to be a cop...investigating a couple of murders.

Stepped up to a woman working out on the speed bag. Introduced myself, asked for a moment of her time and got an exasperated look, a sigh and a flurry of fists as she finished a staccato of blows to the well-beaten leather pod. Looked at me again, grabbed a towel and dried her torso, still looking. Finally draped the towel around her neck and said, "What, you still here? Whatcha' want?"

"Name's Jonas Kirk. You may have heard of me, work with police on homicide cases."

"Nah, never heard of you, Jonas Kirk. Don't keep track of the police much and I don't get involved with homicide. Again, whaddya want?"

"Well, Miss, Mrs...a name?"

"Dorothy Eisner."

"Well, Dorothy, you seem to be well acquainted with the gym to judge by your expertise with that speed bag. True enough?"

"I know some people."

"You know Walter Woods?"

"I do."

"He work out here a lot?"

"Well, if you call walking around in gym clothes and talking to people working out...well, he does hit the heavy bag pretty well from time to time...yeah, he does that a lot."

"What's he talk about?"

"Well, hell, insurance...that's his business...that's what he does. Everyone knows that."

"How well does he do in here...selling insurance"

"About as skilled as I am with the speed bag and just as hard to pin down...talks a lot, gets signatures, seems to give most people some peace of mind."

"And you. Did he sell you a policy?"

"Why do you care?"

"Just helping out the police investigation, Dorothy... and you are being very helpful."

"Well, I like being in the loop about things," she paused, thinking. "Well, you say you and Devlin work together, eh."

"Uh huh, and so did Walter sell you anything."

"Yep, accident and life. Covered for everything now."

"Your husband?"

"What makes you think I'm married?"

"Oops, sorry. Just assumed."

"And you know what that makes you."

"I do. Let me rephrase. Are you married?"

"Yes. And yes, Walter sold my husband and me a nice dual, double indemnity policy. Anything happens to me, my old man can continue doing what he does now for the rest of his life."

"And that is?"

"Nothing."

"You're the sole wage earner?"

"We have a business. He pretends to manage things. I sell, I collect, and I deposit. So, I know where the money is and that's all I need to know."

"So, you're covered. Woods sell any more of those policies, life insurance ones?"

"Oh, I never know for sure. But I saw him talking to that monster man, Steve Gordon long time back...thought I heard some patter there about how it would protect him if anything happened to his wife...and vice versa... he seemed interested."

"Anyone else?"

"Well, yeah, that orange haired thing that started coming in a few weeks ago."

"Geraldine...Geraldine Wright?"

"Oh, yeah. That's it. Boy, she works hard around here but her mouth keeps up with her body. Never heard anyone like to talk and gossip the way she does...not long before she was trying to tell me how to improve my technique on the bag...she's a pest."

"She was buying insurance from Walter Woods?"

"Well, she was sure chatting him up about it. Wanted to know stuff about term, investment, premiums, payouts, physical exams."

"Life insurance?

"Well, that and medical insurance too."

"Hmmm."

"Anyone else you notice getting close to Walter?"

"Let's see, oh yeah, Ingrid Gresham had to listen to him a lot."

"Why was that?"

"She works the bench press...heavy weights, can't really get up and leave while ol' Walter is jabbing her ears with his chatter."

"Was she listening?"

"Well, in a way. Day I saw her, she was working with Steve Gordon. He was sort of encouraging her to give Woods some attention."

"And..."

"And she did. Seemed to listen to Steve a lot, but that would probably be because they work out so much together...both of 'em hogs for the weights...damn strong."

"You mention Steve Gordon. What about his wife...I hear she spends some time in here too, from time to time."

"Yeah, I was talking to Mariel Markham a little and she sees Eleanor come in here at different times, but never with her husband. Some hostility there. Mariel noticed bruises on her face and arms a few times. Eleanor seems to work out a lot of tension with curls and lats... builds upper body strength...and she runs too...runs a lot from what I hear...maybe one of those marathon types. Anyway, no love popping up between her and ol' Steve. That's clear enough."

"Does Mariel chat up Walter Woods at all...interested in insurance?"

"Has to be or he wouldn't spend too much time with her...and he visits with her regularly...here in the gym. Don't know what he does on his own outside time."

"Say, Dorothy, one more thing..."

"I'm about done here, Jonas Kirk. Got to get over to the heavy bag for some fun...what more?"

"Just curious...as a private citizen now...see much drug activity here at the gym...people looking to build body contest muscles, ease through soreness, maybe someone looking to just enjoy a post-workout high from time to time...nothing really criminal...but do you see any of that?"

"I hear stories."

"And..."

"There's a certain pharmacist in town that seemed to spend a lot of time here, the dead guy, what's his name?"

"Jerry Wilcox."

"Yeah. Him. I never saw him here in gym clothes... mostly talking, circulating. Probably some stuff being moved that way. Hate to finger anyone, but Steve Gordon always seemed to stay pretty close to him, and so was Mariel Markham. A pair those two. Once heard 'em talking about the movies, that series they're having at the *Rivoli*... and Steve said something about his home theatre being available in the afternoon...had a collection of mystery movies, he said."

"Remember any other private invitations he may have extended?"

"Nope."

"Really? Hmmm? Private movie showings though, eh. That's news to me."

"Well, maybe you don't get around as much as you think, Jonas Kirk. Anyway, every once in a while Steve invites a whole group of us to see some special movie... maybe three-four times a year...went once...he served sandwiches, drinks, soft or hard, and we had a double feature."

"Learn anything new about him?"

"Well, I learned he loves guns and killing. Even showed us a collector's pair of derringers he had, "Cobra Derringers", he called them. Pretty...and deadly from the looks of them. Asked if anyone wanted to fire them...we might get interested in them for self-protection. No one took him up on that offer."

"How about the movies? Remember any titles?"

"Ummmm...something about a man...Fat Man... Dead Man..."

"*Thin Man*," I offered.

Yeah, that was it...one of those real old movies...don't remember much about it...the other one sort of stuck though, *Chinatown*...that Jack Nicholson film where he gets a nose full...or I guess I should say gets his nose sliced...umpphhh. That really bothered me."

"So, Ingrid. Good ol' Steve has unexpected interests, eh? Movies...old murder mysteries."

"Oh, yeah. He really got into them...wouldn't let us talk or anything while it was up on the screen. But hell. It was a really good time. I remember. Just don't go to many gatherings like that, but if he asks again, I'll try to make it."

I paused. Dorothy had turned out to be a faucet that ran and ran and ran. Told me that Woods had been busy pollinating his insurance hive, that Jerry Wilcox was a regular, polite dealer, but mostly a spectator in the weight room. Steve Gordon, she said, was likely being overly friendly with another drug customer...Mariel Markham. He and she both looked angry...appear to be looking for some way out. And, Steve, he liked old, detective murder mystery movies. Now that last item...Grant and Devlin were going to like hearing that.

I took my leave, asking Dorothy as I left whether she worked out on the heavy weights at all.

"Nah...those are for sissies...big push, oomph...no staying power. I told Steve Gordon that many times. He's fun to visit with, likes local gossip, but that power lifting... ugh...not for me. I like sustained stamina, like runners do. Well, enough. Good talking to you, Jonas Kirk. Go slap someone up and find a murderer out there. Poor ol' Jerry

Wilcox. Harmless. Low life cricket, but harmless. Sad to lose him."

"I'll try to lock someone up soon, Dorothy. You've helped a lot. Maybe check back later."

"Bring your soft gloves, Jonas Kirk. I'll teach you how to hit a moving target."

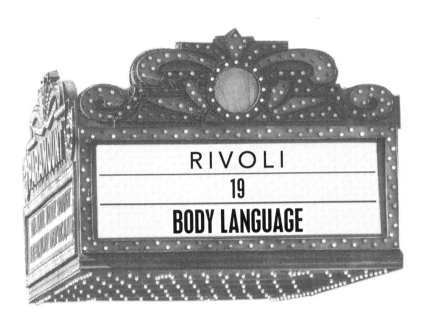

RIVOLI

19

BODY LANGUAGE

Steve Gordon sat in the corner of his music room, sorting through his guitars, seeking one that fit his mood and his song. Finally pulled down his 1952 Martin 000-18, strummed it, tuned it a little, replaced a missing E string and put the capo on the 7th fret, fingered a G shape playing in the key of D and started with a bass-run lead into "Blowin' In the Wind". Pleased, he moved on to "Tambourine Man", and "It Aint Me, Babe", changing the capo and chord shapes for each, dropping the E string to D along the way. Finally, he finished with the fingerstyle version of his favorite, "Don't Think Twice".

Paused, ran the melodies through his head again, then went back to "Blowin In the Wind". Something about that lyric, the inevitability of change appealed to him. He could feel the strength of the chords coursing through his body as he worked the lyric through his mind. Turned him into an instrument powerful enough to define his future.

As the flow of time and the promise of the lyric reverberated, he let his mind begin to wander over to Eleanor. Their marriage seemed to be fracturing against the sledge of misdirected activity, misshapen conversation, mishandled responses to cues for reconciliation. He wasn't sure anymore on how to greet her when she appeared in his space, something that happened only rarely now.

He picked up a set of drumsticks and began to explore a rhythm on the edge of the counter. Relaxing staccato and it kept time to his thoughts. For example, he asked himself, just where was she last night? Today? Da...da...da, da, da, da, dat!

He asked around at the gym yesterday...got some gossip about things, especially from that Dorothy Eisner. Da.da.da.da...dot.dot.si.dot.

So, Jonas Kirk was asking questions. Wonder if he was gonna' talk to Eleanor? According to her calendar she was near Moose Lake on a 50-mile run. That certainly took her out of gossip range. She'd spend her day along country roads where strategically placed stores or stations would give her opportunity to take a potty break and restore fluids. Other than those few intervals, she was running. No other conclusion. That was her way to avoid him, seeking a sanctuary that kindled her spirit. Did it help her? Not sure. Da.da.da.da...dot.dot.dot.

But he became angry just thinking about her. She wasn't there. They weren't talking. He was becoming exhausted trying to work out his frustrations in the gym or revive his spirits here in his music room. Tried to lose himself in mystery movies in his theater, but grew distracted with that. Loose ends. Nice phrase and that was where he found himself. He went back to "It Ain't Me Babe". No, Eleanor, far as he could see, it ain't. Da.dat!

He opened a small black box that he kept in a glass case. Admired his matched set of Cobra derringers, collector items modeled after the 1866 Remington. Picked up one of them, felt its weight, gently tossed it back and forth between his hands as he pondered his little stratagem. Hmmm. He did like holding it...felt compact, weighty, lethal. Nice rhythm. Power coursed through his palm to his gut. On impulse, he loaded it with two .22L caliber bullets. Needed cleaning. Later. Nestled it carefully into a large hip pocket on his trousers. Zipped it closed. Felt good. Made him smile.

Maybe he should ask the cops how the investigation was going. Maybe he'd talk to them with his little two-chamber friend in his pocket. They were so dense. But Jonas Kirk? Now, he was a different matter. Really didn't want him nosing around too much. Nearly finished with his plan. And Kirk wasn't part of it. But...he might be.

Cleaned the studio. Tossed a couple of broken drumsticks...no longer needed. Put the Martin back on his wall and thought about going down to BodyMold. Always something going on there...and he was usually at the center of it. Strength mattered. Well, three deaths down, cops in a low silhouette frenzy. The <u>Gazette</u> kept updating a weekly column reviewing the Marquee Murders as they were now calling them. He puffed and held his pride. A series of homicides and they had a phrase for them. So satisfying! They don't have his name...never will...but they now have a label for his work. Powerful stuff. Careful now. Don't get overly taken with yourself. Close now to the final act. Hmmm, Kirk. Nosy...might be a problem. Picked up his long bow and three arrows. Maybe a good day for practice. Maybe live prey? A little more rehearsal, then he could move toward the finale'. He took his tools, placed them carefully under the metal cover of the bed of the Ram and quietly drove away. Work to do.

Nearly 60 miles north of Woodland Park, Eleanor talked herself into extending the run just a little more. She had become a little more committed to finishing a 100-mile race someday soon, wondered if even that distance was going to mark a step toward marriage stability or a leap toward freedom. Steve was a haunting presence, saying little, watching her carefully, following her from time to time when she ran simple errands for groceries, meds, or even to the gym where she was so well known all he would have needed to do was just ask about her.

Hiding from him at home wasn't easy, but she had begun to manage it better. They talked through the niceties of living, chatted at meals about nothing important, made occasional observations about the goings on in Woodland Park, shared comments about the murders which had scandalized the streets and kept some people closer to their homes.

She laughingly commented that the playbill at the Rivoli seemed to be featuring murder mysteries when the most important unsolvable crime was happening right in its own backyard. Steve just looked at her. No response. Well, that was city living for you, she said. No one ever really knew what was going on in the lives of happy faces and tipsy laughter. Still, he did not react.

She stopped, bent over and removed her right shoe, plucked out a small stone that had found its way inside, retied the strings and started up again. No way to persuade Steve that her time in the gym was just personal improvement. He was convinced that she was seeing someone, and that evening, nearly four months ago now, when he saw her talking to Walter Woods...well that almost led to an explosion right there next to the heavy bag. She smiled, that would have been a disaster... her ol' Gordo knocking Walter Woods around. Probably not an easy task either and all because she wanted some instruction on how to hold her fist when leveraging her body into the big sack.

She managed to lead Steve away, explained her interest in the insurance salesman who knew something about posture, shoulder turns and delivery, reassured him that she was not seeking romantic involvement with anyone, certainly not Woods whom she regarded as a bit of a slick willy whose words were easy, but whose policies were vague. She wanted to find out more about insurance options, she told Steve, and he finally settled enough to comment that she need not worry. They already had their double indemnity policy and that should cover any death issues that ever emerged. But, then maybe they could do something with an expanded health policy, she suggested. Maybe talking to Woods was something they should do together.

She laughed out loud even as her footfalls picked up a rhythm and began to glide more smoothly. After all that hullabaloo with Woods, they ended up taking out some gap insurance to cover medical crises. Steve liked that. Seemed to settle him down knowing that they had made a decision that affected them both. That settled her mood too, seeing that he was a little less hostile and insurance was no longer an issue for them. She laughed with him that one of them would have to die to make any big money come true, and that wasn't going to happen for many, many years. Still the policy was there. Nice to know, eh? She ran.

RIVOLI

20

RISKY BUSINESS

Kirk left the gym thinking about Dorothy Eisner...what she knew, what she repeated, what she circulated in the world of gossip that filled the silences between lifts on the racks and the rat-tat-tat of the speed bag. He was picking up new names along with helpful information about the habits of the gym regulars. Ingrid Gresham worked out a lot with Steve Gordon. Eleanor, his wife, avoided him, but she still liked working upper body weights and had taken up long distance running. Gordon loved film. Gave screen parties. A brute on the weights. A walking power lifter. Might be abusing Eleanor. Had a mutual, double indemnity life insurance policy that was coming into force now, two years after they first signed it. Knew Walter Woods well. Did Steve Gordon hold thoughts that Woods and Eleanor might be having an affair. Were they?

Never any full accounting for the range of gossip that filled rest intervals in the gym. Wasn't his nature to be working out with a collection of dedicated personalities, but he could see how information flows might be helpful to his current issues...find a killer. Wondered to himself how much of his conversation with Dorothy Eisner would make its way through the gym in the next 24 hours. Probably most of it. Might even provoke some backchannel gossip that he could tap into. Might have to visit the gym again in a couple of weeks. Just catch up with the folks. Might even try that speed bag. Looked simple. Didn't think it was. Eisner handled it like a professional boxer. She could give him some instruction, and he thought, that might lead to some more information. She kept in touch with the whole network. Went to bed that evening pleased with his new sources of information, wondering what his visit and his conversational interests might provoke in the minds of others. He couldn't say with certainty, but he was willing to make a small wager that the answer to the serial killings could be found in the gym...somewhere between the heavy bags and the bench press. Yep, he'd go back. Slept well. No dreams.

An unusually cool, July morning eased him awake and he found himself well rested. Did some chores, laughed at himself at the way he liked to keep his space neat... and clean. Left his cabin about 10:00 a.m. dressed in light running garb...Izod shirt, New Balance shoes, short pants...drove his BMW over to Nicholas Park and began an easy two-mile circle jog. He let his thoughts about weightlifters, insurance salesmen and movie screenings tumble gently through his thoughts, his footfalls creating a steady background to his mental wonderings.

Gordon and Eleanor were having marital problems. Everyone in the gym seemed to know and acknowledge that. Both seemed to be fixated on working out their anger on the weights and while Eleanor had taken up long distance running to supplement her work in the gym, Gordon seemed more interested in cultivating his interest in mystery film, ranging from the classics of the 40's and the Hitchcock years to fearsome new realistic flavorings of color coded death, even knife slices of noses to go with lopped heads and deadly gunplay. Well, the two of them might be having marital problems, but that didn't tell him much about a potential serial killer. What more could he scrape out of the sweaty impressions of the gym rats? Anything useful?

He approached a gently sloping uphill, felt his laces loosen as he approached a large box elder and a sharp turn on the running trail. Slowed, then stopped to tighten them up. Bent over, heard the "ssssss" of an arrow, the "thunk" of the wood sending him grabbing for dirt, rolling twice into the loose foliage edging the trail. He froze. No sound. No bird calls. No other footfalls. No chatter on the path. Silence. Still didn't move. Slowly stood up, turned his head to look around and felt the hiss of another arrow, passing by, missing the tree but the feathering of it brushing his ears. Down to the ground again, senses jolting one another trying to sort out the source of danger. Not moving this time...waiting. Finally, the distant sound of a truck starting...heavy duty, he thought. He waited. Its low, guttural engine gradually faded, gears shifting... but no sudden, panicky acceleration. Was that the killer... his executioner...his sudden new nemesis...leaving the scene...or just another jogger having made it to the parking lot, now taking a lightly sweated body home to a shower.

He couldn't tell. Listened more. Just silence and he waited 'til the birds began their uncertain twittering, their chatter growing more confident as the moments passed. Was he safe? Slowly, he rose, quietly moving to the protection of the box elder, edging around it until he was opposite the feathered branch which still protruded, its arrowhead partially buried in the bark. He glanced around to see if he could find the second arrow...nothing. It had disappeared into loose foliage much deeper in the woods.

His mind began to work more efficiently...looked at the feathering on the arrow in front of him...patterned, distinctive. Noticed the length, maybe 20 inches, maybe a little more. Slowly worked it out of the tree and saw death at the end of the shaft...5 inches probably, and sharp edged...honed to cut...and kill.

It took several minutes until he could collect his thoughts enough to admit to himself what should have been obvious. This was no errant arrow from a practicing archer. It was a killer missile, launched from a powerful bow, by a person strong enough to pull a lethal arrow full to its arrowhead.

"Someone's trying to kill me!" he muttered softly. Someone was making a personal objection to his quiet investigation into a series of homicides. He knew it and rejected it in the same thought. He, Jonas Kirk, quiet, thoughtful resident of Woodland Park, a small voice of advice to the police from time to time had become a target...a death target. Was he really such a threat to...a killer? Apparently so, and he felt a sudden, new vulnerability. What could anyone really know of his private parceling out of justice? Nonsense. This had to be about something else. Not retribution. More like a preventative strike. Keep him out of something. A murder inquiry? Those serial killings in the movie theatre parking lot? Was he somehow getting close to something and didn't know it?

That 'THUNK' had such an ugly sound...sordid, dirty and so deeply personal. This was nothing like the distant, subtle threat that Jerry Fields had posed. No. This was open, raw, unequivocal death travelling from a hand to the bow connected to an arrow notched to kill him. The swish that brushed his ears sought flesh, wanted to tear ligaments, tried to pierce organs, let blood flow, empty his reservoir of life energy. Christ! Someone tried to kill him! He tried to conjure anger, a sense of revenge, a parade of resolutions about what he could do, would do, to catch this attempted murderer. Failed. All he felt was fear, a numbness that weakened his limbs, paralyzed his thoughts, left him taking a light panicky series of breaths. Minutes passed.

This was not a good day to die. He didn't envision finding one in the near future, but he had a new sense of what death could bring to his comfortable lifestyle. He didn't like it. Fear tasted dirty. He had peed his pants a little. Was that death? The loss of bodily fluids, of breath and oxygen, of muscle control, mental order...was that it...all gone in an instant?

The thought paralyzed his analytic mind. Kill him? Really? Retribution due to someone, but on this day, at this moment, finding a killer left his list of priorities. He wanted safety, and minding his body movement, he carefully left the friendly jogging trail for the security of undisciplined nature, moving quietly through foliage, listening for a breaking branch, a twig, a rustle. Was he still in the sights of his killer? He ached for safety, scrambled like a furtive rabbit, finding a niche, pausing, making another move...seeking safety and wanting it now...Old Farmer McDonald was out there and Peter Rabbit wanted to get home...right away.

It took Kirk nearly 25 minutes to move himself through the foliage edging the trail back to the parking lot. Quiet there. No other cars. Again, then twice more he looked about, listened. Finally, he moved smoothly and directly to his car, hand shaking a bit as he opened the door, checked the backseat and slid quickly into the safety of his BMW. Locked the doors. Listened. Looked about. Nothing here. He started the motor and quietly, carefully drove away. Home. Safety. Get there. Stay there. Be safe. He wondered in passing if there were a movie at the *Rivoli* that meant something to a serial killer?

RIVOLI

21

SNIFFING AROUND

Roger Blaisdell stood before his office door, admiring the print proclaiming his right to be a practicing attorney. Liked the font, the size of the lettering, the authority it presented. An officer of the law, he thought, and a voice in the court. Ambitions that surfaced in the melee of teenage struggles to see a future finally produced something tangible. Status...and freedom to make his future in a nice Minnesota town where a black face, distinctive but unjudged, remained a curiosity to be examined.

More than 18 months now since he got caught up in that *PumpkinFest* murder sequence and that made him something of a special events person in Woodland Park. Most people probably remembered him for the way he set up the pumpkin launchers and the smashing mess of orange squash that he both created and cleaned up. But more important to him was the confidence that he gathered in the eyes of Chester Devlin and Jonas Kirk.

Searching and finding documents that finally convicted Jerry Fields certainly put him in a different category, and he warmed to comments about his ability to search and assess evidence.

Nice memories. Now, let's see what this day brings. He unlocked his door, wandered into his office, wished he had a secretary and knew that his income would have to expand a little bit more to earn that perk...not a lot more but he wasn't going to run a business chasing debt. Took a look at his desk...couple of wills to complete, one bankruptcy to file, three liens to execute...small stuff and still well within court deadlines. He shrugged his shoulders a bit, wishing that there was something on his plate a little more exciting.

Opened his daily copy of the *Gazette* and saw the headline:

MURDER SCENE NO. TWO
SERIAL KILLER IN WOODLAND PARK?

Silence tells the public that police are sitting on their hands. No clues, no arrests, no theories. But three murders in the Rivoli Parking Lot says everything. Movies may be the pathway to motive. Lt. Devlin has stated, "We are exploring every avenue of evidence and when we have something, we will announce it. The public is not in any danger." But we ask on behalf of the people, without a suspect, isn't everyone in danger?

Take note of that. We have a calculating, evil, genius murdering our citizens...man, woman alike. We are not safe! A serial killer is making fools of the police. We need answers!

Phone rang.

He answered it. "Blaisdell law offices."

"Roger?"

"Right here, Devlin. What can I do for you?"

"You been following those movie murders?"

"I am aware...headless body at first scene. Head shows up in trade for another one at second homicide. *Gazette* says police know nothing. I'm curious."

"Linked don't you think?"

"Absolutely. You find anything?"

"Well, Kirk and Sergeant Oliver Grant have been working it with me. Grant has some questions for the *Rivoli Theatre* that he would like answered; Kirk stumbled across information on insurance contacts with drug customers at *BodyMold*."

"Good to hear. Why would you be telling me this, Devlin...any of these sources a client of mine?"

"Oh, no. Want to know if you'd be willing to take a few search warrants into some businesses here in town. We...Kirk, Grant and I...we think we may find out some interesting information in the papers held by the latest victim, Jerry Wilcox...maybe names of regular customers, eh?"

"My authority?"

"I'll hire you."

"I can do that."

"Also want you to look into the insurance records of Walter Woods. Need to find out what he's selling to whom. Finally, Grant would like you to sort through the invoices of the *Rivoli Theatre*...see if you can find out if the scheduled showings of the murder mysteries are ever changed suddenly...how do they decide what mysteries to show? Figured these three lines of inquiry might keep you busy doing something interesting, eh?"

"I charge, Devlin."

"Of course, of course...what did Kirk pay you for your work."

"He was happy to let me bill him at $100/hour."

Silence.

"Roger, you trying to shine my shoes?"

"Just want you to know how you're spending public money," he smiled to himself

Devlin just went quiet. Mumbled under his breath. Went on.

"Well...I guess there's some kind of premium that comes with someone who can understand all that insurance lingo and at the same time trace film invoices and sniff out drug customers."

"When you say it like that, Devlin, I think I should raise my fee...just a little."

"You're serious about that rate."

"I am Devlin. I like solving murder, but there's a price for justice, eh?"

Devlin sighed. "O.K., come on by. Oswald will have you fill out some paperwork. Please keep this as quiet as you can, Roger. We're really just nosing around and I don't want to disturb anyone unnecessarily."

"Really does sound like a bit of a challenge."

"Just get me some useful information."

"I'm on my way. Tell Oswald to have my papers ready... and Devlin..."

"Yeah."

"Thanks for thinking of me"

"Just get it done, Roger...get results and we may have a long run together."

"Again, I'm outta here. Check with you soon."

"Good. Later."

Blaisdell sat back in his chair and twirled a pencil through his fingers...now here was something intriguing: movie titles, drug distribution, life insurance policies. Bound to be fun. Decided to start with the movies. Picked up his coat, adjusted his tie, and gathered his briefcase. Time for a little drive over to the *Rivoli*.

Opened the door to his Camry. Out of caution (where did that come from he thought), looked into the back seat.

All clear. Settled in, fastened his seat belt and headed over to the movie complex. Turned on the radio.

"So, Roxie...you're saying that to get a truly fresh look, people should slather some cold cream on their face...any brand will do."

"Well sure, Mikie...God knows my skin is as rough as a crocodile...or is it an alligator...one is in Florida, one isn't. How do I know? Eh?"

"I'll check that out Roxie, but one thing for sure is that they don't live up here in Minnesota...I think you can find them in that Bill Haley song...he sorta blended them, don'cha know?"

"Yeah, he did...back to my cold cream, Mikie...I find that it works really well to smooth down little ruffles in my arms, eases wrinkles in my face, generally makes my body feel special. Helps keep a smile on my face."

"Yeah, yeah, Roxie, a smile on your face...well that works for me so long as your head is still on your shoulders."

"And why wouldn't it be, you big galoot?"

"Well, ask that lady what's her name...lost her head there in a parked car at the Rivoli parking lot almost three months ago...now they found her head in another car, same parking lot."

"How'd she look, Mikie?"

"Pretty cool I understand...guess she spent her time grooming in a freezer."

"So, cold cream would not help much, eh?"

"Doubt it, though she's gonna' melt soon enough... might need some skin treatment then...certainly gonna' need something to smooth those ugly scales that must be peeling away from her."

"Yeow, Mike! That's enough ghoulish goulash for me this morning. On a serious note, hear anything about the police solving this crime...well I guess both crimes...they are certainly linked, eh?"

"Gotta be, Rox. Lose her head in one murder scene. It shows up in trade with another. Heady stuff."

"Stop that, Mike! Devlin got anything to say about it?"

"Not a word...but one never knows. He speaks to no one."

"Can't stomach that, Roxie. I'm gonna' take a break and refresh with a soda, maybe some candy...time to close up shop here."

"I'm with ya, Mikie, but remember, I'm Roxie Rochambeau...gotta say my whole name...it's in my contract.

"See ya later, alligator..."

"That would be in Florida, Mikie...(laughing). Next up, Mid-day Notes with Rolf and Ray. We're out'a here."

Blaisdell turned off the radio. Loved to hear Mike and Roxie's little word dance each morning, but noted their jokes today focused on the headless lady and her recently found smile. Fears about her killer were beginning to ease.

Too bad. That might be good for some sick person out there, but it wasn't a path to justice. This wasn't over yet. "A serial murderer." That was the phrase he kept hearing about town. And if a killer could not be identified, no motive found, everyone was at risk. Cops needed to find some answers. Well, maybe he could help.

He pulled into the *Rivoli* multiplex, a bit of a joke really...just four screens, but still, a little more choice than the old days. Parked. Knocked on the theatre doors, asked for the manager and was escorted into the office of Mr. Robert Trapp. Brief introduction as Blaisdell looked him over. He could see his eyes widen a bit when he looked up to see a black man there...could feel Trapp scan his suit, lingering on the tie, tracing all the way down to his shoes. Could feel his resignation, sure this was gonna' be a waste of time.

"Mr. Blaisdell. What can I do for you today?"

Roger briefly explained some of the police interest in the scheduling of the murder mystery series. Asked if he could have a look at the booking slips. No problem there, Trapp responded. Went to his files and sorted through some folders, handed them over to Blaisdell and sat back down in his chair. Motioned with his hand to an adjoining table, "Have a good look...be glad to answer any questions that surface."

Took him nearly 15 minutes, then Blaisdell paused, looked over the papers again, briefly, then glanced toward Trapp. Asked a question:

"I see that the general schedule for the murder mystery series was set up nearly six months ago."

"Oh, yes. That's about right. Need to get permits for those films...hard to book them on short notice."

"According to this series of invoices, you made a request to change the showing of *The Thin Man* and push it back into the lineup. You replaced it with *The Third Man*. What's that all about?

"Hmmmm, did I? Well, let me take a look."

Trapp went through the paperwork, looked into the air a bit, went back to his files and pulled out another folder, looked through it, nodded, then exclaimed, "Ahh, yes this is it."

"This is what?" Blaisdell asked.

"This is the request for the change. Got a typed letter from a local saying how much they looked forward to *Third Man* and they were gonna" be out of town and could we make the substitution. As it turned out, we could and we did."

"Oh. Well, who made the requests?"

"No name...just wanted to give us the idea of how important the film was...we don't get many requests like this, and it worked out, so there it is."

"Any other changes occur like that?"

"Oh, hmmm...well let me see," Trapp responded.

Took him a few more minutes and then he pulled out another piece of paper. Looked very much like the same texture as the first. Also typed.

"What's that?" Blaisdell asked.

"Well, there is another request...asked for a substitute for our scheduled future showing of *Silence of the Lambs* in favor of *SEVEN.* That was a little more tricky as I remember it, but we got it done."

"And how soon do you post listings of the film of the week?"

"Couple of weeks or so in advance. Make final decision week before."

Blaisdell asked for copies of the letters, loaded them into his briefcase, thanked Trapp for his cooperation and left...thinking. *Well, well, well. Someone is trying to influence the showing date of some of these mysteries... are they scheduling anything else...homicide?*

Next stop, Jeremy Wilcox' home, and as it turned out, there wasn't much to learn. Blaisdell walked through the bedrooms, searched the closets, touched up the basement and ransacked the attic. No inventory at home, and the more he thought about it, the more convinced he became that Wilcox was truly a five and dime coke dealer. Lifted some inventory from the drugstore too, peddled it where he could...more than likely steroids...probably at *BodyMold. St*ayed small and safe. Should have stayed out of movie theatres.

Well, might as well end the day over at Walter Woods' sorting through insurance policies. Paperwork. He almost salivated at the prospect of discovering what detailed documents might reveal. Woods answered the doorbell, welcomed him and any inquiries he wanted to make but led him directly down to his basement where he was working out. Took him a half-hour to persuade Woods to leave his free weights and come up to his office. Finally agreed to sort through his business records, but it was all friendly enough...and man, Blaisdell thought, this dude can push a lot of weight, again and again.

Woods sorted through some cabinets, pulled out key index files and waved his arm over them. "Look at anything you like, Roger. If it helps solve those murders, I'm in," and that was all Blaisdell needed. He worked for nearly an hour, then finished up by taking pictures of some key documents, thanked Woods for sharing so fully and left.

"Yo, mama," he murmured to himself, "Devlin's gonna' like this."

RIVOLI
22
TRIFECTA

(Late July)

The marquee blazed a new title, this time with flashing lights: *ZODIAC*. The posters below featured silhouette images of San Francisco landmarks, with a teaser, "FRISCO' SERIAL KILLER STILL LOOSE". Sergeant Oliver Grant took note, squirmed a little in his patrol car as he drove by the Rivoli. The words rankled him. Truthful enough, dammit. The Frisco killings, labeled the *Zodiac Murders* by the press, were unsolved. The series of Rivoli murders were also still open cases. But neither he nor Devlin had received any messages from the killer that could be examined, filed, compared. Or had they?

Were those little typed requests Roger Blaisdell found in Trapp's office the actual evidence they were seeking? They asked for a re-scheduling of certain films for viewing pleasure. No harm in that, Trapp thought. Happy to please his viewing public. But Grant kept thinking, what if the letters were evidence. the connection to a serial killer? He, flaunting film titles to the police, even as he executed murder under their noses in the theatre parking lot. Taunting. Arrogant. That was certainly the dynamic in *ZODIAC*.

And where did they...Kirk, Devlin, Blaisdell and himself...now find themselves. Devlin had sorted through all the forensic evidence and could now add the notes to his list. Blaisdell had visited the Rivoli...heck he found the letters...expect he would report to Devlin on what he found at Walter Woods' home too. Insurance policies that might guide the investigation, eh? And Kirk? Well, he had made the rounds at the gym, had visited with customers found in Jeremy Wilcox's sales book and had identified those who had purchased drugs...almost all of them simply steroids. Wilcox had some other customers, but for the most part, no names, just "hi and fly" hits on the street where he moved some of his product.

So, *ZODIAC*, was now the featured attraction. Grant wondered if Trapp had scheduled it per another request. Put through a call from his patrol car, connected to the Rivoli Office, got Trapp right away. Asked the question, "Say, Robert, is the showing tonight, *ZODIAC*, something you are doing by request?"

"Funny you ask, Sergeant. I did get an unsigned note couple of weeks ago mentioning how much the writer wanted to see this film. They'll think I must have super-powers 'cause it was already scheduled once, then I had to move it to this date cause of some shipping complications. But, yeah, I guess you could say there has been a special request for it."

"Same kind of paper used before, typed message?"

"Well, just by looking at it, I would say it was."

"Great! Save that note, will you. Someone will be by to collect it and add it to the others. I'm gonna' concentrate on a close patrol of the parking lot tonight. Maybe we'll catch a killer."

"Well, that would be good for business everywhere, eh. Cops succeed...marquee predicts killer. Public safe. We all win."

"If it works that way, Robert, yeah, we would all win. I'll check back with you tomorrow...see what tonight brings, eh?"

Grant reported this new information to Devlin, explained his strategy of patrol for the evening and got approval. Official assignment. Backup ready at a single call. Might as well get some rest before an all-nighter, he thought. Drove on home and took a two-hour nap.

While Grant slept, Blaisdell wandered into Devlin's office with a smile and a filled briefcase.

"Afternoon, Devlin. Got a moment?"

"I do."

"Good, want you to take a look at these," and he handed over a thick folder filled with paper forms, insurance applications and approvals.

"What's this gonna' tell me, Mr. Roger-Dodger, the name of the killer?"

"I doubt that, but it is going to give us a lineup of persons who might, I say *might,* have motive to kill."

"And Woods was happy enough to share all of this with you...no demands for search warrants?"

"No, not at all. Very cooperative. Seems to have a real interest in finding out who is creating sudden beneficiaries, 'cause survivors are gonna' be filing claims for payouts."

"So, protect the company's assets by finding a killer... sort of a counter-agent, eh?"

"Yep. You still planning a meeting soon with the others, Kirk and Grant?"

"Yes. This may help. Maybe we'll get some direction."

"Hell, Devlin, I'm hoping we catch a killer. Tired of waiting."

Devlin just looked at him, grimaced, cleared his throat and smiled, "So am I, Roger. So am I."

"Well, give the papers a good read and I'll be happy to elaborate with everyone when we meet."

Blaisdell left, Devlin thought some more. Picked up the insurance documents...stared at them with glassy eyes. Set them aside...would leave blathering phrases to lie there for a time. Maybe tomorrow. Hoped it turned out to be a good day.

And it was, if judged by the brilliance of the sunshine. But there were other ways to measure light, and by Devlin's calendar, the morning, clear as it began, guaranteed nothing.

The call came through 20 minutes after he first sat at his desk, still thinking about putting the case together. Oswald just hollered at him, "Phone, Lieutenant"!

Devlin picked up, heard that voice poking him in the ear.

"Well, Mr. Happy Face, I can't find you at Ole's, so I'm just gonna' have to interrupt your pleasant loafing right at the station, in front of everyone."

"Kirk. Why this call? Where you been hiding? Gonna' to see you this evening, right. You want some breakfast?"

"No need. I've had portions of fruit and yogurt. Just thought I might chat a bit. I've been staying close to home, thinking."

"Why?"

"Got a call from Dorothy Eisner a few minutes ago. She's at the gym, expecting to meet with Walter Woods to sign a new policy that he worked up for her. He didn't show, and she seems pretty upset about it. Guess she doesn't like to be kept waiting."

"Why you?" Devlin asked.

"I have no idea, 'cept we had a great conversation lately about people who are there pumping weights in the gym. Maybe she considers me a new training partner."

"Like she might train you to sit and sip, eh?"

"No, no. Nothing like that. She just seemed friendly. We got along."

"So...again I ask, why this call?"

"Two reasons, Devlin. First, I learned that she must be a hell of a gossip because a day after my conversation with her, I went jogging in the park...nice morning, easy exercise I thought."

"You were mistaken about the weather, eh?"

"No, the weather was fine. I was mistaken about the safety of my run...someone tried to kill me."

Devlin took a breath, his eyes narrowing, jaw clenching and body puffing up a bit.

"Someone tried...WHAT?"

"Tried to kill me, bow and arrow, missed me by the proverbial whisker, sent me tumbling into the ground... damn near passed through my neck. Never heard a thing. Didn't see anyone. Stood up and another feather passed by my head. Few minutes later, I heard a powerful diesel engine leave the parking lot."

"You're sure you're all right?"

"Oh, yes...shaken, that's for damn sure. You know, Devlin, in all our little escapades, I don't remember anyone taking a shot at me, much less launching an arrow. That is not a good experience, and I'm sure it has something to do with the gossip I was collecting the previous day over at *BodyMold*."

"Well, you sound pretty settled now. Still having fallout from it? Think there's any point in going over the site, look for footprints or something?"

"No. But I do think it was a sharp reaction to my nosing around the gym. I snapped the shaft in half and took a good look at the feathering. Evidence worth keeping and a cue to some more gossip. I'll let you know what I find."

"Not to be harsh, Kirk, but what was the other thing on your mind?"

"Dorothy Eisner."

"Why?"

"She wants me to go knocking on Walter Woods' door. I don't want to do that without you. Who knows what his files may give us, and I don't want any evidence compromised by some odd doings on my part. Want to come along...maybe we can have some late breakfast somewhere after we knock on his door, eh?"

"Well, my God, you think this necessary?"

"Food, Devlin, food. I'll be buying."

He paused, felt his stomach turn over a bit. Needed to be fed soon. "O.K., I'll meet you in front of his house... ten minutes."

Kirk stood at the front door of Woods' home, watched Devlin heave himself out of his department Ford. He arranged his belt, stretched his arms a bit, and walked up to the porch, rolling a little as he found his step rhythm. He looked up as he approached. "Ring the bell, for God's sake, Kirk. This is unlike you...waiting for me. You sure you're all right...bows and arrows and all?"

"Just want to do this properly, Devlin," Kirk smiled. He wanted the security of the police and the authority of official law and order. He pressed the doorbell. He could hear it ringing somewhere in the house. Pressed it again a couple more times. No answer. He looked at Devlin. "You hear a call for help coming from somewhere in there...you know like someone has fallen and can't get up?"

Devlin just looked at him, then caught the cue, smiled, "Yes, I do. Break it in, Kirk."

It didn't take much...just a hard press on the doorknob, well, two hard presses, the second one being a bit of a jolt. They walked in, paused. Listened. No sounds. Walked about the ground floor rooms. No sign the bed had been slept in. No sign of breakfast makings. They looked at one another. No loft. Opened the door to the basement, saw a light, detected the scent of sweat, workout sweat, but it was mixed with something else, a sweet, acrid odor that they both identified as urine. All still quiet. Devlin led the way to the bottom of the stairs, Kirk a step behind and there they stopped.

Before them, on the bench, lay Walter Woods. At first glance, his death seemed a simple accident. He had been lifting weights, overloaded the bar, couldn't make the press back up to the rack and lost control of the entire load. It had to have come down on his chest, then rolled down toward his throat, cut off air and despite a struggle, evidenced in his disarrayed workout clothing, he couldn't get the weight to move. Asphyxiation. Looked like it from the stairs.

They walked over to Woods' body and saw more, much more. A small bullet hole right in the center of the top of his head. And there in a cardboard box placed at the head of the rack, they found Jeremy Wilcox's head with a bullet hole of its own. A tragic home accident suddenly became calculated murder. And that tiny circular entry wound looked familiar. Kirk and Devlin looked at each other. Small bore....22 caliber. When? Well, who knew... had to be sometime in the past 10 hours. The Coroner could make that call. What Kirk knew was that there was another murder in Woodland Park. Another message from a serial killer? Bullets and decapitation. Hand in hand? Death was always a weighty burden to lift, but when it was on the menu there were always leftovers.

Devlin just looked it all over, remained calm. Put his cell phone to his wrinkled ear and called the station. "Oswald, Devlin here. We have a homicide over at Walter Woods' place. Send a forensic team and the Coroner."

"Right away, Lieutenant."

Kirk looked it all over again, noted the amount of weight on the ends of the barbell and filed that away. A lot there, but manageable given what he had heard about Woods' work on the bench press. No accident. Not a death at the parking lot behind the Rivoli, but murder nonetheless. It was the same killer, Kirk thought, the headless hunter. But one thing *was* different. Woods still had his head. The serial killer didn't see the need to lop it off. No head to take, no head to leave at a future murder. Was he finished? Wonder what the payoff on all of this was going to be. He looked over at Devlin again.

"Gonna' run all this by the others, eh, Blaisdell, Grant?"

"Damn right...somewhere, somehow, we're gonna' make sense of all of this."

"I agree. Looks like we have a serial killer taunting us a bit. Do we have mystery movies involved or not? Is there a marquee murderer roaming about town, in parking lots, in private homes? Is he my mysterious archer? Eh? Gotta be an answer."

Devlin kept nodding to each question I posed. He was getting warm right before my eyes...saw him bring that right hand into a fist and pound it a bit into his left palm. He was on edge. And I was getting irritated because somewhere out there, a killer was wandering around, leading us in a circle or daring us to find his target.

Finally, Devlin growled. "Right you are, Kirk. You go think about it all someplace. I'll handle everything here and meet everyone at my house tomorrow. I'll ask Geraldine for her home-made pizza and I'll fill the fridge with a case of *Modelo*. We gotta have enough information among the four of us to charge someone. Have to."

Kirk gave Devlin an exaggerated thumbs up, then a formal hand salute, smiled and stepped quickly up the staircase. He didn't know why, but he believed that somehow, they were going to find a killer...soon. They'd better. He didn't like being used for target practice.

RIVOLI

23

DUETS

Kirk reached out, half asleep, touched her back, ran his finger down along her shoulder blade and relaxed. Wasn't quite sure why Sharon Cunningham had decided to take him to her bed, but a few weeks with her had begun to mold him into a creature of comfort. His days were less about looking for something to do and more about enjoying what they might do together. She wasn't really interested in biking, hiking or swimming. And he had not usually found much pleasure in strolls, conversation, and speculations about things of little moment about town. Homicide yes. He could charge his batteries to find a killer. But living without crises, enjoying the comforts of calm, learning new touchstones with her in bed. Well, these took his mind...and his body...into a different comfort zone.

She stirred. moaned a little, felt her body warm and relaxed. She felt his hand traipsing across her back.

Remembered last night and smiled. She wasn't sure yet just where this might be going, but it was certainly not evaporating. Their talks, to her great surprise, had begun to touch on aspects of Kirk's life new to her. He had deep seated insecurities about the death of his parents... especially after learning that the accident hadn't been a matter of chance. And his view of what he was supposed to be doing in life continued to focus on solving homicide, working with Devlin, being helpful to the community in an informal way, even as she immersed herself more in the structure of the social hierarchy.

She continued to find deep satisfaction in working with Cold Stone Charity. Victoria Blessing seemed to know every person in Woodland Park with income below $20,000 a year and put the touch on those needing a tax deduction as though she were their accountant. And, she herself nearly had her real estate license, pleased to let Alice Goodwin take leadership for the Altar Society. Visits with friends, especially Geraldine, kept her feeling lively, and although her romance with Ahmed Hassan had finally faltered, she was by no means through with love. All she had to do was turn over and look into those blue eyes Kirk flashed from time to time, and she knew her tummy would contract as she shuddered a little. Morning love? No, not today. She continued to face away from him as he spooned her gently.

No matter. She wanted to talk.

"Jonas. You've been pretty quiet about these killings going on. Not like you. Have anything to share."

He surrendered to a truce on sex for the morning. "Well, yes," he continued to stroke his finger alongside her ribs, loosely held her breasts, wandered nowhere in particular, "We seem...that is Blaisdell, Devlin, Grant and I...we seem to be focusing down on a killer...one who is strong enough to commit the murders and at the same time one who is thoughtful enough to want to taunt us with movie titles and killings that can be connected to some of the plots in the movies."

"And where is that taking you," she asked?

"Well, I think that we'll know more after we meet and find out what Blaisdell got from Woods in the way of insurance information. But I've begun to think that there may be more to learn from the movie series...there are clues there."

She thought for a few moments, then spoke as though thinking aloud. "You know, Jonas, when I was in India preparing to leave, for those not quite believing Father Lockhart's passing was a natural death, there was plenty of speculation. Some whispered that he may have insulted local political figures. Others pointed to his distancing from the poorer communities. Still others found his trips to Rome a cue to failure. But no one saw what was right before them...my relationship with him...so close and yet so visible if one just looked. And that was the key to his death. Personal pique. Sometimes, people get so caught up in trying to make sense of something that they overlook the most sensible idea of all...the most direct line to a murder."

"You think there is a simpler, more powerful explanation as to why these people are being killed?"

"Well, I'm not sure if an alternative theory is really simple, but it does seem to me you guys are grinding on a theory that demands a rather complicated movie explanation...just something to think about I guess."

"Hmmmm," Kirk paused. He had too much respect for Sharon's handiwork in life to ignore a few tips from the spotlight of reality. Maybe it wasn't the movies that paved a trail. Maybe he, Devlin and the others, were all in a stage show. Gonna' think about that.

"O.K. Now what's next in our day?"

"Not what you're thinking. I'm spending the mid-day at the Altar Society and Alice Goodwin. Then I'm lunching with Geraldine."

"Ah, Alice Goodwin," Kirk smiled, chuckled. "She still working with the Bishop as closely as ever?"

"Ah, yes," she replied as she softly rolled out of his arms and rose to the shower. "Still there and still full of amusing misunderstandings of simple sentences because of her poor hearing."

"Let me hear one," he smiled.

"Oh, sure. I recently asked her if Bishop Eggert did his own taxes before he filed. She answered me saying, "Yes, he keeps all his faxes, written in his own style.""

"Wonder what the IRS would say if they interviewed Alice about her taxes sometime," he laughed.

"I think they would mark her *'accepted as filed,'* Sharon smiled, shook her hair loose and went into the shower.

Geraldine finished cooking his breakfast, sat down with coffee to keep him company while he ate, mumbled and wrestled with his thoughts.

"So, Chester, what are you thinking about this killer you have on the loose. I can tell you there's a lot of chatter out there about how incompetent the cops are... no arrests...all these deaths. Got any ideas at all?"

"Gonna' just follow the evidence, Maizie. You know, I just love to arrest people...but it's not always an easy choice. Can't go wandering off the road...can't just invent stuff to close a case."

"Yeah. I understand, but for my money, the answer has to lie over at *BodyMold*. Drugs are sold there. From what you say, the killer has to be someone pretty strong. Just need to hone-in on one of those muscle guys...I would have said Walter Woods, but not now. But there have to be some others. I know when I chatter about in the gym, the name Steve Gordon comes up from time to time as the most powerful weightlifter in the place. Dorothy Eisner also mentioned to me that his wife Eleanor spends a lot of time in the weight room...terrific with dumbbells and arm curls...maybe she's close enough to her husband to know something. She certainly doesn't like his collection of killed animals hanging on the walls, or bows 'n arrows dangling from some of the ceiling... or his array of rifles and pistols. Maybe Eleanor could be pressured to talk about her husband a little more. What do you think, Chester?"

"I think those are all good thoughts, Maizie," he pondered. "I'm getting together with Grant, Blaisdell and Kirk this evening and we're gonna' hash it all out. Thought I'd bring them over here to relax. Think you could make some of your pizza and stock some beer."

"Oh, sure. I'm having lunch with Sharon Cunningham, but then I'll shop and load the place up. Love listening to you work through evidence with Jonas and it'll be nice to meet Officer Grant and visit some with Roger Blaisdell. Sure, I'll have the place stocked and ready."

"That would be great. Now, I'm gonna' get through my day and hope that no one else shows up asking for a Coroner."

Devlin rose, went to hug Geraldine goodbye for the morning, then remembered...wiped his mouth of jam and breadcrumbs...and gave her a quick kiss. "Maybe this time next week, I'll just take the day off and we can see what a drive down to Winona can do for our spirits...just like Old Times, eh."

"I'd like that Chester," she laughed, and her orange hair shook a little. "I'd like that a lot."

It was a rare morning, Eleanor thought, when the two of them were in the house together, but here it was, and she was not quite sure how to maneuver through breakfast and get out of there. Coffee made, she was poaching eggs when she heard him walking softly in

from the bedroom. She glanced over. He was still in his robe, slippers in place. Maybe she could get fed and gone before he started into anything.

"Eleanor, damnit, when are you going to start settling down and staying home!"

Ooops. She wasn't gonna' make it out of there this morning without more threats, tensions. She lost her appetite.

She turned off the burner, pivoted and faced him. Casually sipped her coffee and looked at him. He waited, beginning to puff up a bit in anger. She had a thought. New approach.

"Steve, you know, you're right."

His head jerked up and he stared at her in some disbelief. But she went on. "I've been gone too much, too often. We need to spend some quiet time together... not shouting, not threatening... just listening and talking. Now, I have to leave tomorrow and drive up to Duluth. You've heard me talk about a 100-mile race from time to time. I've been training a lot for it, and I know it's taken me away from any chance to work through our problems. But, let me get through this and I'll take a break from all the running. I saw yesterday that there's a new mystery at the *Rivoli*. You might enjoy it while I'm gone. Then, I'll spend a few weeks staying home, maybe sort things enough that we can keep this marriage together. What do you think 'bout that?"

He continued to just stare. *Took some time digesting what she said. Capitulation? Was she finally beginning to see the light. Gonna' become the woman she was when he met her...quietly engaging, smiling, eager to please, sharing time watching mystery movies, even willing to go to target practice when he fired rifles or practiced his archery. That always made him feel good. There he was, the knowledgeable partner who could make weapons talk, could protect his household, could provide meat for his freezer and be happy with a compliant wife. Was she willing to reconcile on those terms? Well, that could change his plans. He stared at her, something in his memory reminding him of her hard body when it was receptive, clinging, challenging. Maybe it could happen.*

"Well, hell. All right, Eleanor. That sounds a lot more like the woman I married...and I know that I've been a bit of an ass for months...just can't understand what's changing you...or who you are changing for, but what the hell, I'll leave all of that for later. O.K. You go off on your 100-mile run to prove to everyone that you really are crazy. I'll stay here, watch some movies, shoot some archery, hit the weight room down at *BodyMold* and just hang out. You say there's a new mystery at the *Rivoli* I haven't seen. I might take a look. When you get home, maybe we can start putting our marriage back together, eh?"

"Steve...that's just great of you. Just need to finish this run and then we'll concentrate on us. Be back within a week...take a little time to recover...path goes from Duluth down toward Moose Lake and then back again. I'll be thinking of you," she paused and smiled, "see you soon, hon". He glowed.

"You really feel that way, Eleanor?"

"I do, hon. I really do. Just another week. OK. love?"

He almost purred.

Didn't really matter. She'd had enough.

Geraldine circled the room, "You boys all have enough to eat? New brew anyone?"

They all four nodded yes, little murmurs of satisfaction coming from each of them. Devlin looked around, settled on a conversational strategy.

"O.K., one by one, I want each of you to tell me what you have found, what you suspect and what you know. Roger, let's start with you."

Blaisdell took a moment, configured his opening line in his head, looked at each of them and began.

"O.K. First the movie playlist at the *Rivoli*. The film each week is usually scheduled far in advance. In three instances, it was modified at the request of the viewing audience. Similar paper in the notes, a typed request. I suspect our killer was setting up the film showing to coincide with a murder. I know that there is a corpse for each of these films mentioned."

"Can I jump in here, Roger?" Grant spoke quietly.

"On the subject of the movies?"

"Yep."

"Go."

"I've reviewed the films that played the night of each of these murders. In every instance, one could find links between a message in the movie and the victims we found. In the first one, the double murder, the film *The Third Man* cautioned us that we had a third man missing too...our killer. *Seven* the second film, focuses on a climactic scene with a delivered, severed head. Connection obvious. The third film, *Zodiac,* featured a killer taunting police about their impotence in catching him...a message to us. And we haven't caught him yet."

"And you suggest what?" Devlin asked.

"I suggest that we are being played by a reflective, skillful killer who knows film and isn't afraid to flaunt it."

"O.K. I'll buy that. Now what more do you have Roger."

"Well, my next visit was to the home of the dead pharmacist, Jeremy Wilcox, and I found nothing. Strictly small-time dealer. His death appears to be a simple taunting, as suggested in *Zodiac*."

"Anything more?" Devlin kept the talk moving.

"Finally visited Walter Woods and he was happy enough to let me look at any papers I wanted. Found a number of policies written to people who frequent the gym, but one in particular caught my attention."

"Well, good...go on."

"You didn't look through it yet, Chester?"

"Nah. Tired of little type and big words. Figured you could explain it to all of us...go ahead."

Blaisdell took a breath, then shared, "He had a signed and executed policy for Steve Gordon and wife, Eleanor. A double indemnity policy and it had two features that I found unusual."

"Steve Gordon?" Devlin interrupted. "Isn't he the power lifter you mentioned, Kirk. Workout mania man at the gym. Strong as a horse, obstinate as a mule, dangerous temperament. Same guy right?"

"Yep" Kirk answered.

Devlin went on, "Well then, Roger, what were these two unusual features?"

"First, it was a $5 million policy. Huge, but Walter said they both wanted it to be a large payout cause if anything happened to one they wanted the other to be without financial worries."

"They paid their premiums on time?"

"Yep, for two years now."

"What else?"

"Well, it included the usual exception for death within six months, but it's a double indemnity policy. Survivor's going to walk away from accidental death with $10 million."

"Does 'accidental' include being a victim of homicide?"

"Well, sure, so long as the killer isn't one of them. But this policy calls for instant payout. Company assumes risk to challenge the distribution later."

"Unusual in your experience?"

"Yes, very unusual. And when I say instant, I mean it."

"Well, how?" Devlin looked hard at Blaisdell.

"The way I read the fine print in these documents, the specific payout...$10 million...has been set aside by the company and placed in a trust account naming Roger OR Eleanor as the active owner. Upon public notice of the death...take note of that phrase 'a public notice', the $10 million is directly deposited into a numbered Hong Kong account. Even a death notice in the *Gazette* would trigger the policy."

Devlin seemed skeptical, "A simple report of death... even if it were murder?"

Blaisdell had an answer, "Yep...even if it were a notice in the newspaper...in a news column. Any public notice and the account is activated for the survivor. Now, if one of them were convicted of murder the company might sue to get its money back. But that could be cumbersome and uncertain depending on where the survivor ended up living. In the U.S., no problem, but there are places around the world where one could live a long, happy life with $10 million."

"Think there is motive there, eh?" Devlin smiled.

"Absolutely."

"Why Hong Kong?" Grant asked.

"No extradition?" Devlin asked.

"Well, it used to be that way...changed recently, but there is iron-clad secrecy on all accounts. Makes a great landing spot for a distraught surviving partner, eh? Whatever the purpose, they both agreed to it, as did the insurance company...and charged a hell of a premium to service it," Blaisdell answered.

"But both are living and working. So, peculiar policy. No suspects."

"Yes...lots of gossip about their marriage being in trouble, but right now, they're both heathy and active."

"Well, good enough," Devlin moved on, "Apart from observations about the Gordon's marital happiness, anyone have a theory for the murder of Woods?"

Blaisdell paused, thought a moment, "He may simply be the next victim in a series of killings taunting the police. But maybe Steve Gordon finally became convinced that Woods and Eleanor were having an affair?"

Devlin grimaced, "Back to the Gordon's marriage, eh? Can't we move on from them?"

"Maybe not," Kirk commented, "Gordon has a fixation on murder mysteries. Has a private collection, even throws a movie party for the gym rats from time to time. Moreover, didn't you mention to me, Devlin, that there were fibers found at the murder scene of Jeremy Wilcox, both on the floor and of course near the headrest. Those fibers might match karate outfits. Steve has several."

"Anything more, Kirk?"

"Well, he is arrogant. Seems convinced that he controls the world, has a deeply aggressive personality. Plays the guitar well and he's strong enough to loop a wire, maybe a guitar string, around the neck of Lisa Leslie and Wilcox. Break a drum-stick and he has two handles to leverage decapitation, and broken wood easily trashed.

Geraldine chimed in, "And his wife, Eleanor, has complained to friends at the gym how much she dislikes his arsenal of pistols and rifles. Maybe that includes a derringer. Chester says the first murders came from a .22 caliber bullet, as did Wilcox' death...no shell casings...fits a derringer."

No one complained about her joining the conversation. She felt warmed.

"So, the Gordon's are going to be lead characters in our little real-life movie, eh?" Devlin gave in.

"That's a plot that seems to compel a good look," Blaisdell commented.

"Motive, Kirk? Jealousy sounds plausible," Devlin commented. "But if so, how'd he get into Woods' home? If Woods is in bed with Eleanor Gordon, why would he let Steve in? No break in. Opportunity? Was Gordon in the house at all?"

"Oh, I think he was, Devlin. Best way for Woods to deny an affair with Eleanor would be to ignore it. If so, he has no reservation in admitting Steve, a client. They work out in the gym together from time to time. But...I'm not sure we're talking about marital jealousy. I'm still thinking Gordon may have gone over to Woods' home as part of his serial homicidal game. Much like the Zodiac killer. Different methods of death, different settings. Even Jeremy Wilcox's murder was a little different from Lisa

Leslie's. She was shot, beheaded. Jeremy was strangled, then shot and beheaded, and now Woods is simply shot and left on the bench. Steve could have just stood above Woods...to spot for him while he lifted a heavy load... then put a .22 bullet in his head when the bar was on his chest. It stayed there. I'm still thinking that Gordon has to be one of our main targets, eh?"

"Let me pop in here, if its O.K.," Geraldine looked to Devlin for approval.

"Sure, what'sha got?"

"Well, comments about Steve from Eleanor. She told me he loads lots of his harvested meat into a large freezer...probably enough room to stash a severed head for a while, don't you think, Chester? She's afraid of him. Never see her in the gym with him...she pushes a hell of a lot of weight...gotta be really strong in the upper body, but they work out separately."

"Well, that all adds to the little pile of speculation we got goin' here," Devlin commented. "Anything else. Was Woods having an affair with Eleanor?"

Grant cleared his throat. "No evidence of that at all... but I suspect she knows that Gordon's been watching her when she is in town...which is not often. Doubt she would be linking up with Woods or anyone else with that pressure on her."

Grant paused, then continued, "It just seems to me, looking at the tie-ins to the films at the *Rivoli*, that he's a disturbed serial killer...maybe acting out in reaction to a failing marriage and all the suspicions of betrayal that surface when that happens. Probably feels that we think he is just a strong bozo and won't see him for the psychological mess he is."

"Well, I wouldn't argue with that," Blaisdell responded, "But what about that huge joint insurance policy. Did that two years ago. That's the act of a thoughtful man. Was he setting up a possible payout to himself. That policy makes Eleanor a possible long-term target, eh?"

"I've wondered about that," Kirk commented. "But the killer left Woods' head in place. That might suggest that he has tired of the game and has no victim in mind for a new cranial exchange. We may have lost him."

"Or," Grant reminded, "He may simply be varying the pattern...as per *Zodiac.*"

Silence within the house.

Devlin, cleared his throat, spoke softly. "Well, I think I'm gonna' bring Steve Gordon in for questioning tomorrow. Probably our prime suspect, but still...just a person of interest. Don't start any gossip about him. Let me visit with him first."

The confab broke up, everyone feeling that they had contributed to the conversation, all of them comfortable with targeting Gordon. Gonna' be interesting to see how he reacts to a summons, they thought. Devlin cautioned them again, "We'll do it all quietly tomorrow about mid-day and see what he can tell us. May take a day after that to look over his responses and measure them against our known facts and our speculations. But you'll all hear from me before we make any formal arrests."

RIVOLI

25

RUN FOR FREEDOM

He was gone when she arose, late morning, feeling drugged. Too much sleep. She was usually the one to greet the morning and make the coffee. Not today. Looked over to the counter...fresh pot waiting for her. Note on the counter read:

"Breakfast at Ole's, then workout...Devlin wants me to come over to chat a bit. You been complaining about us any? I warned you about that. You can go ahead and take the Ram up there like you asked. Plenty of room to store your stuff. But this is gonna' be your last race...you said."

Well, she thought, Steve might find that he was in more trouble than he thought. No matter. She had told him she was leaving today for the 100 Miler and Duluth was a distance. Need to get started. She thought ahead. The winding trail country would cap off a training regimen that had kept her busy for several months. Figured that she could get up to Duluth today, get settled tomorrow.

Race began at noon the following day...maybe 30 hours to run it and then a day to recover. Come on home. Five days...less than a week...plenty of cover.

Took out a pen, wrote a brief note, placed it on the kitchen counter.

It read: *"You'll have to deal with Devlin without me. New film at Rivoli like I said...violence...you might like it. Off to Duluth and 100-mile race. Thanks for the Ram. Not running away...just running."*

That should do it, she thought. Piled stuff into the truck, picked out some snacks for carbohydrate loading, loaded a good supply of water, an ice chest and a couple of extra pair of shoes. On impulse, she went to the weapons room. Never know...out there on the trail... running. Carrying a little pistol could provide serious self-protection. Opened the case that held the derringers. And stared. The matched pair...gone. What the hell? Where could Steve have put 'em?

She looked about a bit more, her mind sorting through possibilities...where could they be? Began to make connections. Suddenly grew shaky. Just how important were those derringers to him? Would be like him to carry one around...she had seen him cradling it from time to time, tossing it lightly between his hands, holding it like it comforted him. Was it a murder weapon? Her husband...a serial killer? Who was next? Why would he have both pistols on him. What was he up to? What could that mean for her? That stopped her pacing. What could that mean FOR HER?

Had another thought, a long one. Looked around a bit, picked out another weapon. Not noon yet. Plenty of time. Called *Singapore Airlines*. Booked the flight. First Class. It might all work out. Getaway time.

For Steve, the morning had gone well. Nicely paced, good night of sleep. Eleanor still sleeping. Thought about the next few days, Her running that 100 Miler circle from Duluth to Moose Lake and back. He knew the route reasonably well from deer hunting. Plenty of time to welcome her home.

Made a mental schedule. First stop, Devlin. Time to shed the derringer. Couldn't sit still for an interview with that piece of evidence in his pocket. But he might have some fun with the cops if they wanted to arrest and search him. Smiled.

Grabbed his cleaned karate garb, pocketed both Cobra derringers and squeezed himself into the Yaris. Grimaced at its lack of power, lightweight steering, jolting ride, cramped seating. How did Eleanor put up with it? Parked a bit away from Ole's so as not to be seen in such a piece of trash. Light meal. Drove by the Rivoli. *Killing Season* on the marquee. Never heard of it. Not a classic murder mystery, just an action conflict between a shooter and an archer. New to him, but maybe a nice diversion.

Next stop, the gym. Worked out, showered, dressed, dropped his cotton karate garb into the trash bin outside the house. Done. Took the fresh, unfired Cobra derringer and put it into his pocket. Disposed of the other one in the big ol' Mississippi as he drove to Devlin's. What a joke this could be, he thought. Devlin maybe searching him... it could happen...and they would jump for joy at finding a .22 derringer in his pocket. And then ballistics would tell them they were all wrong. He smothered a laugh. They were going to look pretty silly when they had to return it to him... and keep searching for a killer. Maybe he would suggest that they check the *Rivoli* for clues.

Next stop after Devlin...maybe the movie, then a night of rest. Tomorrow, he'd be obvious about being in town. That would keep the cops calm. When Eleanor got back home, he could finish the dance...time enough...a week or two. He'd make a new request to that dunce Trapp for a specific film playbill for Mystery Murder Night. Then, a new death. Another marquee murder and that would end his problems. He smiled.

Headed for the station. Walked in quietly, asked Oswald to see Devlin. No problem. Invited into the Lieutenant's office and there he sat, expecting to chat a bit about what the police might have found about the death of Walter Woods. Maybe they wanted him to vouch for the integrity of his insurance practices? Maybe they wanted to learn more about his prowess on the heavy bag at the gym? Who knew?

Devlin knew. He sat there with a frozen face and a hot series of questions. He grilled Gordon more than four hard hours, taking him through each of the murders, his knowledge about them...about movies...about weapons... about weights...about martial arts clothing...his alibi for nights in question...finally about a gossiped rumor of Woods' affair with Eleanor. All the while, Steve sat calmly, smiling gently on one point or another, periodically placing his hand into his deep pocket. Cradled the safe derringer, fit it into the palm of his hand. A talisman. He breathed easier.

Sure, he admitted, he was a little jealous about Woods...but that was an issue between him and his wife... they would work it out. Woods was his insurance agent after all. Trusted him to do his financial work.

Karate uniform? New lightweight one. There in his locker. Have a look. No problem.

Did he possess a .22 pistol? Well, yes, a matched set of Cobra derringers, collector's items, though one had been missing for some time. Maybe Eleanor was carrying it for self-defense when she was out running and didn't tell him. *Felt that weight in his pocket. Smiled to himself. These cops...so dense.* Devlin was welcome to go through the house at any time.

When asked about his whereabouts the nights of the murders, Gordon stated he was at home, alone...didn't know where Eleanor had been. Hell, maybe she was out there killing people. She worked the weights...could probably lop a head off with no trouble. *Let Devlin mull that over a bit, he thought.* He listened intently to some questions, dismissed others with a wave of the hand, laughed easily on occasion, appeared to be in every way, innocent and certain no one could prove otherwise.

My God, Devlin thought. This guy has every qualification to be named the murderer, and no alibi for the nights in question. Putting a lot of suspicion on his wife, Eleanor. But he is absolutely confident in recounting his movements, his knowledge, his innocence. Didn't panic. Seemed to know he was untouchable. So confident, but not arrogant. Nothing really solid to use as a basis for an arrest. Was this a movie script of its own? Reminded him of the Ted Bundy interviews. Gordon, remarkably convincing, spoke in the same quiet, innocent conversational technique that Bundy used, an overlay to the serial killer beneath.

Along about 5 p.m. Devlin sent him back onto the streets. Don't leave town, he cautioned, and Gordon walked out a free man. Too antsy to go home now. Edgy, but strangely fortified by the way Devlin backed off when he offered up Eleanor as a suspect. Let him and his friends grind away on that for a while.

Now what to do? Eleanor off to Duluth.

Hmmm. A movie? Thoughts of popcorn along with the hotdogs and mustard he could get at the snack counter. Feed his face and watch a new film.

Checked the marquee...*Killing Season,* with John Travolta and Robert De Niro. Hadn't seen it. Posters featured Travolta posing with long bow and a hell of a long arrow. What would this be, archer vs rifle, two rivals seeking to kill one another? Well, it looked interesting... up close and personal. Bought his ticket and went inside.

Found his seat...touched the derringer, his little friend, cleaned and unfired for months, both chambers empty. What a pair they made. Good will flowing everywhere.

It was dark when he emerged. Terrible film. Travolta never worse. Di Nero neck deep in film garbage. Took a strong sampling of the cool air. Dismissed the film from his thoughts. Popcorn was good. Felt alive. Almost smiled at the thought of Devlin and his ideas of who killed those people. "Serial killer?" he told Devlin. "You need to start looking for deranged people...maybe even my wife...but not me." Not Steve Gordon.

He kept those thoughts revolving in his mind as he walked to his car. Patted his pocket to reassure the Cobra that he was still attentive. Still thinking of the way that Devlin seemed so certain about him, he opened the door to the Yaris, went to plop himself into the driver's seat.

Found it a little tight. Squeezed in. Reached down, grabbed the spring release under the seat and pulled it, at the same time using his feet on the floorboard to slam the seat back as far as it would go.

Even as he wondered how it had lost its position and came to be set so far forward, the five-inch arrowhead pierced his back, ran through his chest, slicing his heart, setting off the arterial flow which no amount of hope could control. He gasped, gripped the wheel, tried to turn, tried to open the door, tried to cry out. But as quickly as he could think of each possibility, he knew there was no way out. No detective could touch him for murder, but someone else has. A last thought. "The bitch is rich."

Kirk's cell buzzed and he lifted it off his breakfast bar and checked the number. Devlin. What now? He answered and the words came spewing out.

"Dammit, dammit, dammit, Kirk! Can you guess what I'm dealing with right now?"

"Indigestion?"

"No, no, no, dammit! I'm dealing with another of these marquee murders...and you'll never guess the victim!"

"Am I supposed to try?"

"NO! I'm gonna' tell you. It's our suspect Steve Gordon! Found dead this morning in his car in the *Rivoli* parking lot. Chest run through with an arrow...apparently fixed to kill him when he moved his driver's seat back to fit his comfort setting."

"Not too comfortable now, is he?"

"Don't think he cares, Kirk. But I do. What the hell... where are we...where are we going now? I want to arrest someone, and I got no one to put in cuffs...what the hell!"

"What movie was playing?"

"Something called *Killing Season*. Some kind of mano-a-mano contest between two ex-military guys...Travolta and DeNiro...bow and arrow against a rifle I think. Just chatted briefly with Bob Trapp the manager and that's what he told me. Said it would leave tonight."

"Where's Oliver?"

"On scene now. Jesus, Kirk, is there no end to this? If Gordon wasn't our serial killer, who is? Got any answers for that?"

"Not yet. Let's hope Eleanor's safe. Then, we'll see everyone this evening at your home. O.K.?"

"Yeah...what the hell. No other options right now...just hope you can sew a circle around this mess."

"Tonight. Seven o'clock?"

"Done."

RIVOLI

26

BOX CANYON

They distributed themselves around Geraldine's living room as randomly as a small sack of marbles emptied into dirt. Each had thoughts about how they had wobbled in targeting Steve Gordon as a serial killer. But if not him, then who? Where had they gone wrong? As before, Devlin started.

"I can tell you all that Gordon was killed by a long, steel tipped arrow, propped against the front of the rear bench, aimed at his torso on the other side of the driver's seat. When he adjusted it for comfort, he essentially killed himself. But I can also tell you that we found a .22 derringer in his pocket."

A collective gasp, and Devlin let the excitement build, finally quietly popping the bubble with a quick comment. "The derringer is not the one used to kill the other four victims. Unused for months. Chambers cleaned and smooth. Ballistic evidence excludes it."

A collective sigh.

"Well then," Grant finally commented, "If not Steve Gordon, then who the hell is our serial killer? We're still at sea on that. Is he now just the fifth victim?"

"And that is now the question," Devlin spoke quietly. He looked at Kirk. "Got anything for us?"

"I'm stunned, Devlin, and scrambling. I thought there was a simple answer."

"A simple answer? Eh? What would that be? EH?" Devlin shouted, "Nothing about this whole mess is simple...it's just damn complicated. So what's the simple answer, Kirk, eh? Come on...what'cha got?" Devlin look hard at him.

Quiet.

Grant broke the silence. "Damn good question. Simple is hard to come by. These victims are so unconnected... hell, I'm not sure how one can make them out to be casualties of a personal grudge. But a serial killer often just chooses random victims...unconnected to one another...a person that just catches his eye. Wants the conversation to be more about his cleaver killings than the possible evidence leading back to common features of victims. Linking murder to movies works."

Quiet.

Kirk broke it. "Bear with me here. I'm thinking as I go. We have been selling ourselves the idea that we had a serial killer using movies at the Rivoli to taunt us, a psychopath."

"Well, yes," Grant commented, "Each of those films had some scene or a theme connection to the murder and in every killing, we find a head...lost head, found head, strangled head, bullet in head. Even today...an arrowhead. All connected. A psychopath linking film and death, taunting the police, eh?"

Blaisdell joined in, "But our suspected serial killer was not the film expert, Steve Gordon. He's dead. So, what was he...just another random victim? And if so, who are we looking for?"

Devlin jumped right in on that. "Yep. The way that derringer was zippered in his large side pocket...couldn't have been placed there without moving the body...and that didn't happen...so he was carrying it, but it turns out to be the wrong pistol and as you say Roger, Steve Gordon turns out to be just another victim. So, who is the killer? All done or still in town...in full murder mode?"

Grant cleared his throat, "The question is simply, 'who killed Steve Gordon?' Answer that and you have your serial killer."

Kirk let the silence reign for a few seconds, then thought out loud. "Maybe our killer was working through a series of homicides just to murder a particular person?"

"Well, if Steve Gordon is the real target," Geraldine blurted, "Who wants him dead? Who the hell could that be...killing four people just to get to this muscle-bound piece of crap? Eh? My God! Who in the hell could that be, Kirk?"

Kirk spoke quietly, "Well, it could be his wife, Eleanor. I'm thinking out loud here, but let's examine the idea. Their marriage was a mess...she sometimes appeared at the gym with bruises on her face, probably threatened to leave him. If his psychological profile follows clinical models, he likely blamed her for provoking his abuse... she didn't understand him...probably little or no sex in their lives...her absences were both insulting and embarrassing...and...nothing clinical about this, she was worth a lot of money if she were dead...but so was he."

Blaisdell grinned, "True enough, that policy made a survivor worth a fortune if the other were in a box."

"Money and murder, eh? Think she saw him moving in her direction? Beat him to it?" Grant asked.

Kirk answered, "Well, she was the one being abused... maybe she just saw murder as a way out, and took a stairstep approach to getting rid of him."

"Eh?" Devlin sounded interested

Kirk went on, "If she planned a series of killings which we attributed to a serial murderer, and concluded with the murder of her husband, that insurance policy would keep her comfortable for years. She knew neither restraining orders nor even a divorce would likely keep her safe from him."

"You know," Devlin commented, "He kept mentioning that she was not at home on the nights of any of those murders. Figured he was just blowing smoke. Thought that he was playing a killing game with local film offerings and trying to put blame on her...but maybe he was telling me the truth."

"Right. Maybe she created her own reality film." Kirk paused. "Given his abuse of her, she may have just been playing the long game on survival."

"So, how could she make it happen?" Geraldine could not restrain herself.

Kirk had an answer, "She had seen the marquee advertising the mystery film, *Killing Season*. Saw the arrows in the graphics. Timing perfect for her. Plenty of those around the house, and I noticed that it had the same feathering as the one that nearly killed me. She knew her weaponry."

"Strategy?" Grant asked.

Kirk paused, "Well, we'd have to look at the case of dual derringers that he had...Dorothy Eisner once commented on seeing them when Steve held that big film party out there. Guess he liked to show off his various weaponry... part of his passion. With respect to his death, it could be Eleanor planned to use the derringer once more and have us believe that the serial killer was still active. Clearly then, Steve would become just another victim. Then, the killings would suddenly stop, and she could stick around and enjoy her money."

"So, this lethal arrow wasn't her original plan?" Devlin interjected.

"I'm thinking not. If she went to get the dirty derringer to use on him when he came back to the car after the movie...and found that it was not there, that both the pistols were gone...well, that was different."

"How so?" Devlin was following along closely, demanding a logic that pointed to a killer

"Well, if both derringers were gone, that meant that Steve suspected her as the serial killer and checked the box that held them. One had been used. By whom? Figured it was Eleanor. Knew that if he dumped the used derringer and kept the clean one, that little double-eyed piece of metal in his pocket would confirm his innocence for the murders. But it also opened the door for suspicion to fall her way for all of them."

"Why?" Geraldine fixed her eyes on Kirk, shook her orange hair.

Kirk paused thinking, "If a pair of Cobra's existed, and the one in Steve's pocket was clean, Devlin here would ask who had the other one...the weapon that killed four other people? Eleanor had household access. Lived in a tense marriage. Her alibi for Steve's death is a 100 Mile race, essentially out of sight. And if she killed him, maybe he *was* the real target in her killing of the other four...a stairstep kind of vengeance, eh?"

"And where is the dirty derringer, Kirk?" Devlin asked.

"Well, most likely it is with her on her run or she has tossed it somewhere on her way out of town."

There was a long pause as thoughts reconfigured themselves in their collective minds.

Finally, a voice.

"She's running a 100 miler up in Duluth isn't she?" Geraldine asked.

Blaisdell answered. "I'll check that out...right now," and he made a call. Room quiet. Blaisdell spoke softly, "Yep, need to confirm one runner...an Eleanor Gordon...I see. Yep. No, no need to worry. Just wanted to see if she had checked in. No problem."

He put the phone away, commented, "She didn't show."

"Well then," Grant asked, "Where is she?"

"Just run out the time-line, Oliver," Blaisdell wasn't smiling. "If she set the arrow that killed her husband, she has now had a 24-hour head start on us. I'm willing to bet a free ticket to the *Rivoli* that the *Gazette* printed news of Gordon's death in today's issue. That will trigger the special provisions of their insurance policy. The company's trustee will have moved Eleanor's money to a sealed account in Hong Kong. Her long-distance run will likely pause there and continue on to a country without an extradition agreement with the U.S."

Grant grimaced. "Well, damn. So that explains the double bill at the Rivoli."

"What's new there?" Kirk asked.

"I drove by the theatre on the way over. The marquee and posters were being changed. Travolta's gone. New mystery double feature. I asked Trapp about it. He said that an anonymous letter writer had sent a cash gift and asked him to schedule the two films for a five-day run.

"What are they, Oliver?" Kirk asked.

Grant looked around the room, then said, softly, "*GONE GIRL* and *DOUBLE INDEMNITY.*"

"My God!" Geraldine was stunned. "So, she decided that if Chester didn't hold Steve for murder, she was gonna' kill him sometime this week. Sweet Jesus!"

"Yep," Grant spat it out, "And unlike Barbara Stanwyck in *Double Indemnity,* she didn't hesitate to finish him off. Think Eleanor is laughing at us right now, eh? EH?"

"Oh, yes she is," Devlin growled. "And she isn't trying to get away with one murder. She trying to get away with five of them. My God! This is a dangerous woman! Can we catch her...or is she truly gone?"

The *Gazette* answered that question the next day.

"GONE GIRL KILLER RINGS GONG IN HONG KONG"

Eleanor Gordon, the serial killer who murdered her husband, Steve Gordon, has narrowly escaped the long arm of the law. In a herculean effort, Lieutenant Chester Devlin sorted through a mountain of misdirection and hidden evidence to get an arrest warrant for her, but his efforts to detain her in Hong Kong failed by hours. She was on the island briefly, did some banking, then departed by private jet bound for Yap, one of the larger 600 islands in the western Pacific that make up Micronesia. Authorities say that given reports of Gordon's physical condition and stamina for long distance racing, combined with the life insurance payout upon the death of her husband, Steve Gordon, she could enjoy living on any one of the 65 habitable islands indefinitely.

Bank Asia confirmed that the account held in Eleanor Gordon's name in Hong Kong had been emptied into the Bank of The Pacific. She has her money and Micronesia has no extradition treaty with the U.S.

According to local attorney, Roger Blaisdell, the Freedom Insurance Company noted that without her conviction for homicide in an American court, it could not sue successfully in Micronesia to force return of the money. Without extradition, Blaisdell commented, there is no Eleanor Gordon and no trial. "She's free but she is boxed in. Micronesia is now her home."

Blaisdell expressed regret that Woodland Park would have to wait some time to levy justice for four earlier victims and for Steve Gordon's death. But there was no doubt. Eleanor Gordon was the Marquee Murderer. And, he noted, "There is no statute of limitations on homicide."

Local case cracker, Lt. Chester Devlin, quietly confident of the department's position, reports that, "Sergeant Oliver Grant has been following these murders for months, certain there was a tie to the marquee mysteries shown at the Rivoli. There was. Like the story in <u>Gone Girl</u>, she made it appear that her husband, Steve, was a murderer. We no longer believe that. Our serial killer, Eleanor Gordon is far, far away from justice but Woodland Park can rest easy tonight," he said. "It is safe. We are all safe."

RIVOLI

27

PILLOW TALK

Kirk unfolded the paper, lay it over the nude body of Sharon Cunningham as she relaxed on her side, on the bed, facing him, occasionally touching his hip with her fingers. He smiled, caressed her forehead with his hand and commented, "Disappointing that Eleanor Gordon got outside the reach of law, eh?"

She paused before answering. "I have mixed feelings about that, Jonas."

"Oh?"

"I think you all were on the right track at first... targeting Steve as a serial killer. He fits the profile... personal enmity, emotionally erratic, egocentric, powerful and interested in blood sports. But he certainly didn't kill himself. So that means Eleanor did him in."

"Yep...and?"

"But her killing Steve doesn't mean she was a serial killer. Nothing about her personality as you describe it to me leads one to that conclusion. Think about it, Jonas. Every killing, except Steve's, was accompanied by a pistol shot. If she had the dirty derringer, why not use it and then get rid of it. No, she didn't have it. My guess is that he got rid of it as he felt Devlin getting closer. Carried the clean one to protect his innocence."

"That derringer again," Kirk answered lazily, "When are we gonna find it...examine it?"

"I think it is gone forever, Jonas. Drag the Mississippi. Beyond that, don't you think it was Steve Gordon pulling the bow on the arrow that nearly killed you. Hard to believe that Eleanor had that much strength."

"Hmmm, yeah, could be...but some people in the gym mentioned that she used to try to please Steve by shooting target practice, and she was known to move the weights around easily."

She paused, let her hand move over to Kirk's shoulder.

"You mentioned the heavy-duty engine that pulled out of the parking lot after you dodged the arrow. Eleanor drives a little Yaris...no reason for her to be steering a big Ram out there to draw a bow on you."

"Can't argue with that, Sharon."

"And I'm curious, Jonas, when you think back about the big pow-wow, who suggested that Steve Gordon's killer had to be the serial killer. Who said that?" she asked and touched his stomach.

"Hmmmmm, now stop that... ahh let me think...uh, let me see, oh, yeah, I think it was Oliver Grant, and it captured the mood of the moment."

"And what is Sgt. Grant invested in...a theory of linkage between the movies and the murders. For him, every killing needs to fit that connection to justify his analysis. And there it is, Travolta and DeNiro on film, battling arrow to gun. Someone had to die to fit the movie. Eleanor could make sure it was her husband. An arrow fit the movie. Consistent link between film at the Rivoli and death in the parking lot. It certainly persuaded Grant she was the serial killer."

"Well, yeah, fits his theory, but not long after, I bought into the idea, suggesting that Eleanor could be using a stairstep series of killings to get to her husband. What we didn't have was the murder weapon, the derringer she used."

"The one someone put in the Mississippi," Sharon commented. "Probably Steve Gordon himself...and that still allows him to be the serial killer. Any doubts about that conclusion, Jonas?"

"Not 'til now."

"Is there a simpler explanation, do you think?"

"I think you're going to offer me one."

"Jonas, I think that somewhere in that big pow-wow, your little group of detectives got going on the wrong path. When I run Steve through all of these scenarios...your near death...a violent killer of four disparate persons...a figure fixated on murder mysteries, a man obsessed with violence, a collector of guns...my conclusion is that he is without a doubt the serial killer and Eleanor, knowing his anger about their relationship, an anger that she mirrored...saw herself as the next victim in line. She just got to him before he got to her, eh?"

Kirk grew quiet, remembering the comment that Grant made, "Find Steve Gordon's murderer and you've found your serial killer."

But had they? Sharon's analysis was correct on every known point. Why should Gordon's death whitewash his possible responsibility for the four other killings? And he, Kirk, was the one who had offered the idea of a stairstep series of killings which only Eleanor Gordon could have wanted to commit. But Steve might have had a similar plan.

Suddenly, in a way distinctive from his earlier conversations with Devlin and the others, Kirk felt the certainty of his logic collapse. He drew a deep breath, became distracted.

"What are you thinking, Jonas?"

He was thinking that Sharon's view was clear, simple, and fortified with logical truth. Stripped down to the essential elements in these deaths, Steve Gordon had to have been the serial killer and Eleanor was likely his next victim. She may have felt it and beat him to it. As Sharon had mentioned before, murder was usually personal. Steve's death certainly fit that description.

"Sharon...you're making a lot more sense than our group did."

"Well, who led them in the wrong direction, Devlin? Maybe Grant?"

Kirk paused, thought at some length and the silence began to weigh on them both. Then, haltingly, he spoke.

"I think I did. I accepted Grant's thesis that whoever killed Steve Gordon was our serial killer. I was wrong... really wrong. How did I get carried away with such a complicated answer to a simple series of deaths? I'm feeling a little queasy right now, Sharon. Maybe it's time I get out of this murder business."

Silence.

Finally, Sharon spoke, "You've solved a lot of homicides, Jonas. Not a bad thing to miss on just this one."

"You saying that we should reopen the case...get a legal finding that we sorted it out wrong?"

"Oh, God no! Little good would come of that. Five people including the serial killer are buried and gone. Eleanor wants to live freely in Micronesia. Fine. She destroyed Steve, but he would have murdered her."

She paused. "Settle, Jonas. Maybe someday, we'll have a chance to talk to Eleanor about it all...maybe a vacation in Micronesia...island hopping...who knows, eh?" She smiled.

Kirk felt his spirits rise. "Oh, a Pacific explorer are you...looking for Amelia Earhart and finding Eleanor Gordon. Well, she's outside our jurisdiction now...I draw the line there and start a new one here," and he moved his finger from her throat to her breasts.

"Sometimes, Jonas," she smiled as she moved her hand out from under the *Gazette* and reached for his hip, "it's best to ignore local gossip and read what's underneath the headlines."

"You lookin' for another byline to fill?"

"I'm thinking about another movie to view."

"Oh?" he asked, "What's playing at the *Rivoli*? *Blazing Saddles*?"

"That's the right film for the moment, Jonas. Mount up. Just be sure you finish up with the fine print," she whispered. "I don't want to feel like yesterday's old news."